"I came back to try and mend our marriage."

Katrin heard Ruark sigh as he went on. "I had a plan worked out in my head— how I would wine and dine you, buy flowers, ply you with memories of the past, the good memories. I was going to charm the socks off you."

"Only the socks?" Katrin asked.

He laughed and bent to kiss her. "No, not only the socks." He raised his head and became serious again. "I intended to suggest we start again. Instead—wham! You told me we were already divorced."

"You never wanted a genuine divorce?" Katrin asked, daring to hope.

"Not then."

She shut her eyes. "And now?" she asked carefully.

"Now things are different."

Books by Elizabeth Oldfield

These books may be available at your local bookseller.

Don't miss any of our special offers. Write to us at the
following address for information on our newest releases.

Harlequin Reader Service
P.O. Box 52040, Phoenix, AZ 85072-2040
Canadian address: P.O. Box 2800, Postal Station A,
5170 Yonge St., Willowdale, Ont. M2N 6J3

ELIZABETH OLDFIELD

dragon man

Harlequin Books

TORONTO • NEW YORK • LONDON
AMSTERDAM • PARIS • SYDNEY • HAMBURG
STOCKHOLM • ATHENS • TOKYO • MILAN

The Chinese Zodiac is a twelve-year cycle which has no counterpart in the West. It is believed that to a great extent, the year in which a person is born will determine his characteristics, and often his fate. People born in the Year of the Dragon (1928, 1940, 1952, 1964 and 1976) are sensitive and sincere, never flattering. Indeed, at times their honesty can be brutal. Strong minds ensure they are resourceful and clever. They can also be short-tempered and stubborn. Great warriors, blessed with courage and indefatigable energy, are often born under the Dragon sign. The Dragon represents the greatest celestial power, and symbolises life and growth.

Harlequin Presents first edition July 1985
ISBN 0-373-10805-2

Original hardcover edition published in 1985
by Mills & Boon Limited

CHAPTER ONE

KATRIN shot a glance back over her shoulder. She was laughing, but her deep violet eyes had taken on a rebellious glint.

'Hey, just remember who makes the decisions around here! You stick to peddling your diamonds and leave me to run the model agency.' The drawing pin poised between her thumb and forefinger was rammed home. 'If that's not too much to ask.'

'But it's imperative you submit entries. Every agency in Singapore will be falling over themselves to take part in the competition.' Her stepbrother inspected the glossy-paged brochure again. 'Have you taken note of the details? They guarantee whoever becomes the face which sells DeSouza cosmetics an annual income of well over a million dollars. And don't forget that if Pivotelle manages to sponsor the winner, we'd rake in fifteen per cent. Plus the publicity generated would bring a tidy slice of extra business our way.'

'*Our* way?' Katrin started to challenge, but changed her mind. 'Any chance of winning must be a snowflake in hell's chance,' she argued, thrusting her hands deep into the pockets of grey leather trousers. 'There'll be a deluge of entries, and not just from Singapore. The contract is the most coveted one in the entire Asian beauty business, so from Japan all the way down to Indonesia girls will be interested. Every model who can mobilise two eyes, a nose and a mouth, and who isn't exactly covered in acne from head to foot, will dream of becoming Miss DeSouza. Personally I feel preparing a special portfolio and building up hopes is a sheer waste of time.'

'Somebody has to win.' Oliver absorbed her fighting stance, the spots of indignant colour in her cheeks. She was a tall, slender girl. Strictly speaking she was not beautiful, but when she smiled she deceived everyone. 'You could enter yourself,' he suggested.

Katrin sighed. 'Think again.'

'Why?' he protested. 'You have clear skin, fine bone structure, and those huge eyes of yours are a knockout.'

'Thanks for the compliments, oh shortsighted one, but as far as modelling goes, you're way off the mark. DeSouzas require a fresh bud, not someone who's already clocked up a quarter of a century. Also they won't choose a European face, not when the TV commercials and magazine adverts are geared towards South-East Asia. An almond-eyed beauty will be required.'

'Then give Roselind a spin.'

'No, I won't. Her nose is too flat.' She noticed her stepbrother had begun studying the small print and eyed him for a moment before turning to concentrate again on the cork board with its selection of photographs. Sooner or later Oliver would be bound to read the name of the international advertising agency which was organising the competition, and then what? She must be on guard. Katrin repositioned a head-and-shoulders shot of an innocent-looking brunette, the type of maiden who would have sewed samplers in turrets in days of yore. 'To be frank, the only model on our books right now who'd have a realistic hope of scooping up the Desouza contract would be Lisu here.'

Oliver strode across the office. 'Pretty little thing,' he agreed, peering at the photograph.

'She's half-Chinese, half-American, so not identifiable as any particular nationality just vaguely Oriental, which would suit DeSouzas' markets. She's also straight from school, and has the most exquisite ivory skin you ever saw.'

He frowned, thick blond brows meeting. 'She reminds me of you. At least, how you used to be before that brainstorm struck and you had half your hair chopped off, then frizzed what remained.'

Katrin flicked her fingers through the torrent of dark tumbling curls which fell to her shoulders, laughing at his disapproval. 'You must keep pace with the times, Oliver.'

'But your hair was down to your waist,' he protested, then he sighed. 'I still remember the first time I saw you. Felix had brought you round to have dinner with my mother and me at the big house. You were seventeen. You wore a white broderie anglaise dress, and satin ribbons were tied in your hair. You were very demure.'

'But I'm not now?' There was a tease in her smile.

Po-faced, he studied her. 'Demure girls don't paint their eyes like that, nor march around in leather pants and waistcoats with precious little underneath.'

'Considering there's a long way to go before you reach forty, you have a very stuffy streak,' she chided. 'Just because you choose to wear a sober Savile Row suit and plain white shirt day after day, you think everyone else should be equally conservative. Well, not so. In half an hour's time I'm off to compère the fashion show at the Regent, and I've no intention of standing behind the microphone in one of the classiest hotels on the island dressed like a frump.'

'There's no danger of that,' he retorted, unable to stop his pale eyes from skimming the vee of her waistcoat where a tantalising glimpse of firm tanned breasts was revealed. 'Felix would never have approved of your outfit,' he grumbled. 'But on the other hand, Ruark would consider you a very tasty dish.'

Ruark. The most emotive word in Katrin's personal dictionary took her unawares. From the moment her stepbrother had picked up the brochure she had been on edge, yet she had not expected a mention so soon, nor in this context. She winced. Ruark's name carried too many echoes of conflicting feelings. Oliver, she suspected, may have purposefully dropped her ex-husband into the conversation in order to test her, and by reacting she had failed. She tried for an offhand shrug.

'Neither Daddy nor Ruark are here any longer, so?'

'The businessmen lunching at the Regent will ogle you.'

'Fantastic! All women thrive on being ogled, it's far more beneficial than vitamin pills.' She was flippant, but when Oliver curled his fingers around the top of her arm in protest, she sidestepped, wrenching free. She didn't like him to touch her. Come to think of it, she didn't like any man touching her these days. Katrin crossed to a cabinet and withdrew a buff-coloured folder.

'Maybe if I flutter my eyelashes I'll be picked up and land myself a dinner date? It would save me the bother of cooking when I get home.'

'I'll take you out to dinner,' he put in quickly.

'Just joking. I'm keeping Arlene company this evening, and for the next few evenings,' she added, resorting to subterfuge. A little of Oliver went a very long way. He could be impossibly righteous, and critical. Now it seemed incredible they had managed to co-exist so peaceably in the same house for almost eight years.

'Please yourself.' He sounded hurt, like a misunderstood adolescent, but then he glanced again at the photograph on the wall. 'If you consider this girl might be suitable for DeSouza's why don't you submit her name?'

'Because Lisu Ho is a timid little mouse. Winning a major contract, with all the attendant razzamatazz, would be her idea of purgatory.'

Oliver looked unconvinced. 'But if she's so lacking in confidence, how come she's a model?'

'Due entirely to a battle-axe of a mother.' Katrin grimaced. 'Mrs Ho frogmarched Lisu in here one day to enrol for our various classes, and now she's pushing like mad to have her prowling the catwalk. Mrs Ho is desperate for her daughter to hit the big time, like overnight! But Lisu has a long way to go. Indeed, I doubt very much if she has the emotional spunk to make a career in modelling. All the signs are that her nerves will let her down and that she'd be a disaster, either on stage or working for DeSouza.'

'What a very convenient get-out,' he declared.

Her head shot up. 'Meaning?'

Oliver returned to the desk. 'You think I haven't managed to work out the real reason why

you're so determined not to put names forward?'
he jeered, shaking the brochure in her direction.

'Please tell me.' Katrin acted cool, though in
truth she felt she had much in common with a
fish on a hook, well and truly caught.

'Because the advertising agency acting on
DeSouza's behalf happens to be the one which
employs a certain maverick Aussie. The guy who
walked out and left you flat—Ruark Lencioni!'

She iced him over with a look. 'Don't portray
me as the jilted wife, Oliver,' she warned. 'I'm
not, and you know it. The situation wasn't that
simple.' An empty sensation gnawed at her
stomach, but she refused to pay any attention.
'To return to the point—I agree my relationship
with Ruark has influenced my decision that
Pivotelle shouldn't become involved in the
competition.'

'Ha!' her stepbrother said in triumph.

'But not from any emotional aspect,' Katrin
continued steadily. 'Read the rules and you'll
discover employees of both DeSouza and the
advertising agency, *and their families*, aren't
allowed to sponsor models. As Mrs Lencioni, I
can't put Lisu's name forward.'

'Katrin, my precious, may I point out that your
divorce came through almost a year ago, and that
you haven't set eyes on Ruark since God knows
when?' Oliver said, using cold logic. 'Your
connection with him now is zero. Why you cling
on to the Lencioni tag defeats me. Discard your
wedding ring, revert to your maiden name, and
forget that damned man ever existed. Be
independent.'

'I am.' She hoped her face didn't show how
much the facts wounded, even after all this time.

'And speaking of independence, let me get my cheque book and——'

'Not so fast,' he interrupted.

'Fast?' She gave a sharp laugh of incredulity. 'The money to pay back your loan has been lying in the bank so long that it'll soon have gathered dust, and yet you keep stalling.'

'Katrin, we're family.' He gave her that indulgent smile she knew so well. 'I was only too happy to help. Besides, the money represented more of a gift than a loan.'

'Not in my view. If you'll just agree to the amount of interest I've added, then I can write a cheque this very minute. I'd like to have everything squared.'

Oliver made an adjustment to the knot of his dark blue tie. 'Leave the matter for the time being, there's a good girl. I'm not in the mood. I'm off to Antwerp in a couple of days' time, and I'm tied up with preparations. When I come back we can come to some arrangement.'

'But I don't want an arrangement,' she said impatiently. 'For years I've stashed a portion of Pivotelle's profits away ready to pay off the loan, and now that it's available you keep brushing me off. All that's required is——'

'Don't stampede me, Katrin.'

The set of his jaw warned her they could be heading for a lengthy harangue, and on Monday morning Katrin was far too busy for that. She decided she would deal with the debt her own way and take no notice of Oliver and his prevaricating.

'I hope the boutique don't spring any last minute changes,' she said, leafing through the folder which contained details of the outfits to be

modelled that lunchtime. 'This booking at the
Regent is our debut, so I'm desperate that
everything goes smoothly.'

'Are we there for a week?'

'No. I managed to twist the management's arm
and land a contract for the entire month,
Mondays to Fridays.' She grinned, so pleased
with what she had achieved that this time she
bypassed her stepbrother's possessive use of 'we'.
'And there's a bonus because a week on Saturday
the girls are booked to appear in the Regent's
ballroom. Ten models are to have their hair
styled by top local salons, using products being
launched by a big German company. The
evening is a gala affair. First there's a grand
buffet dinner, then a choreographed mannequin
parade in which the girls show off their topknots,
and finally dancing. Should be fun. Everybody
who's anybody in Singapore's fashion and hair
scene will be present. I believe people are
clamouring for tickets.'

'Sounds like you pulled off quite a coup,'
Oliver commented, as the telephone began to
ring.

Katrin nodded happily and leant to lift the
receiver. When she recognised the voice, she
pulled an eloquent face.

'Good morning, Mrs Ho. And how are you?'
She listened for a while, circling a finger to
indicate how her caller was grinding on and on.
'Lisu isn't really ready for catwalk exposure yet,'
she managed to insert. 'I've explained before how
turning a pretty girl into the perfect model can
often take twelve months. Lisu must learn to
relax.' She was interrupted, and only had a
chance to speak again when the woman took a

pause for breath. 'You've heard about the hair promotion? Yes, it is very prestigious and your daughter does have lovely healthy hair, but——' More Donald Duck quacking came from the phone. 'Leave things with me, Mrs Ho,' she said, forcing her way into the conversation at last. 'I'll speak to Lisu when she's in tomorrow morning for her class.'

Katrin had replaced the receiver and was reaching for her folder, when the door opened to reveal a statuesque strawberry-blonde in her late thirties.

'Hi there,' the woman grinned. She was wearing a vermillion-coloured chemise, saucily side-splitted in such a way as to frighten even horses. 'Are you ready to leave?' Her hazel eyes slid to Oliver, who had become very stiffbacked. 'Not broken up a tête-à-tête, I hope? You're looking quite the debonair gent, Ollie. Have you just broken out of Pierre Cardin's shop window?'

Regally ignoring the verbal swipe, he retaliated with one of his own. 'Still blooming I see, Arlene. Off to model outfits for the fuller figure? Or is it the older woman? I never can remember.'

'Touché,' his opponent grinned, quite unperturbed.

Katrin grabbed the folder and her shoulderbag, deciding it made sense to exit before they crossed swords in earnest.

'Let's go. I'll see you on your return from Antwerp,' she tossed at her stepbrother as she and Arlene headed out.

'Antwerp?' The blonde stopped in her tracks. 'Doesn't Antwerp have a kinky red light district where the hookers are put on show in shop windows?' She looked doubtful. 'No, maybe I'm getting mixed up with Amsterdam, or could it be Hamburg?'

'I wouldn't know,' Oliver replied, his mouth looking as if his lips had been sewn together by tight stitches. 'Red light districts aren't my scene.'

'But they're all part of life's rich embroidery,' Arlene grinned. 'Check Antwerp out, Ollie, old mate. Check it out.'

'You've probably ruined his whole day,' Katrin chuckled as she stopped her car at the traffic lights. 'You know how much he detests being called Ollie.'

'And he'd run off shrieking with his hands crossed in front of him if a strange woman so much as winked at him,' Arlene declared, making them both laugh. 'I don't know why, but his puritan streak always brings out the worst in me. I hear myself becoming more cringingly outback Australian by the second, and we both know his opinion of Australians.'

'We do indeed,' Katrin said with feeling.

The midday sun dazzled, so she searched beneath the dashboard for her dark glasses. She tried to remember if Oliver had found Australians so hard to take before Ruark appeared on the scene, but could find no evidence. As she pushed her sunglasses on her nose, the noisy pawing of engines on either side of her warned a green light was imminent. She slipped the gear stick into first. The traffic was nose-to-tail, each of the three lanes chock-a-block, and every single driver considered himself, or herself, to be Grand Prix material. Katrin knew if she didn't leap from the mark in the first split-second when the light turned green, she would incur the horn-blaring wrath of those behind her. Foot poised above the acclerator, she noticed a gaggle of Japanese tourists. By weaving hotfoot through the stationary traffic, they were dicing with death. Judging from the number of plastic bags they carried, they were out on a shopping spree of a lifetime. What had they bought? Singapore was a duty-free port and there were rich pickings to be had. Would they fly back to Tokyo bearing jade rings or fragrant sandalwood fans, cameras or twenty-four hour suits?

The 'go' light flashed and the Japanese leapt *en masse* for the pavement. There had been only centimetres to spare, for the traffic ripped across the junction and into Orchard Road like a lion pouncing on its prey. Orchard Road was always busy. This up-beat vein of the city was a wide thoroughfare, studded with gardens and white-icing tower blocks and elegant hotels. There were shopping precincts by the dozen, each boasting more variety, more bargains, than the last. Tall roadside trees cast strong shadows in the sunshine, and fountains showered noisily on forecourts. Less than a hundred miles from the equator meant the island's climate was tropical—hot and steamy all year round—but the imaginative use of greenery helped make daytime temperatures more bearable.

'Is Ollie still uptight about your move into your own apartment?' Arlene enquired, as Katrin drove expertly along.

'Very much so. He can't understand why I wanted to leave the big house. If he's told me once that we're family and should stick together, he's told me a thousand times. To hear him speak, you'd think we were Hansel and Gretel alone in the big bad world.'

'But you'd never set eyes on each other until you were seventeen and he'd reached his late twenties.'

'Exactly. And now that both his mother and my father are dead there really isn't anything to keep us together, certainly not in each other's pockets. We have very little in common.'

'But he's still possessive?'

'He tries!'

As they neared their destination, they lapsed into silence. Most of Katrin's life had been spent in Singapore, yet she invariably saw something new when she was out and about, something which intrigued. The unique jigsaw of races, Chinese, Malay, Indian and European, had provided the tiny island with a vivid jostle of lifestyles. Look one way and you came across saffron-robed monks lighting joss sticks in temples, look another and there was a millionaire in a Mercedes. Look behind and you found a wrinkled old Cantonese woman between the shafts of a wooden handcart, look ahead and——

Katrin looked ahead and saw the Regent Hotel, three slender skyscrapers linked by golden-roofed pavilions. A hundred years ago this land had been native jungle, but architects, builders and gardeners had created one of the most impressive hotels in the whole of South-East Asia. Beneath the marble-pillared entrance, dark-skinned doormen in crimson velvet tunics awaited their arrival.

'You landed a plum when you negotiated for Pivotelle to do shows here,' Arlene praised. 'This is some place. The doormen look like they belong in Aladdin's cave, and I'm crazy about the thirty-foot waterfall and banks of bougainvillea they have in the lobby.'

'Let's just hope nobody disgraces us by tumbling off the catwalk,' Katrin grinned, as she switched off the engine. She climbed out of the Ford and passed the keys to the car valet, who gave her a ticket in return.

'They won't,' the blonde assured her. 'Not when they've been trained by you. Oliver might kid himself you need to be cossetted, but you're coping fine.'

'Am I?' she wondered.

The older woman flashed a perceptive glance. 'As far as Pivotelle's concerned, there are no problems. Okay, emotionally you're still picking up the pieces, but take it from one who knows, you need years to recover from a divorce. And your father dying at the crucial time didn't make things any easier.'

'Thanks for sparing me the usual platitudes.' Smoked glass doors slid apart and they walked into the hotel. 'Everyone else says I'm young and resilient, and how lucky it was that no children were involved.' She pulled down her mouth. 'Most folk expect me to bounce back like that cat in *Tom and Jerry* cartoons. He gets flattened by an express train, does a quick cartwheel, and he's as good as new.'

'Mmm, Ruark was a bit like an express train.'

'Jet-propelled!'

'You can't blame people if they expect you to bounce back,' Arlene suggested hesitantly. 'You do tend to project an aura of bright-eyed optimism.'

'But that's all it is, an aura.'

There was a wisp of melancholy, but then she caught sight of a cluster of sloe-eyed girls and Katrin grinned. 'Good, everyone's on time. We're using a store room adjacent to the kitchens for changing,' she explained when the girls, high-heeled and willowy, gathered around. 'Which means you won't need to walk far. As usual I'll arrange the outfits in running order, plus accessories, so there shouldn't be any snags.' She stepped across to a mahogany sidetable. 'Touch wood.'

Touching wood worked. Ninety minutes later Katrin could bask in the knowledge that Pivotelle's debut had been a complete success. Her girls had strolled up and down the T-shaped catwalk in the centre of the luxurious green and gold restaurant, modelling the clothes with sophisticated flair. No-one had tumbled. Instead everyone had floated, buoyed up by the applause which had greeted their appearances. Now each model had one last change before massing on stage for the grand finale.

'Shee Lah again, looking like Princess Tiger Lily in a brilliant yellow flower-printed two piece,' Katrin enthused, bringing the microphone to her lips. 'In a climate like ours natural fabrics are a must, and this stunning ensemble is in pure silk.'

She watched the Chinese girl parade, gave information concerning the gold sandals and gilt jewellery Shee Lah was wearing then paused, waiting for her to depart. The arrival of the next model provoked a stir of interest, particularly among the male diners. Here was Arlene, who had firmly established herself as favourite. Thirty-eight in years and hip measurement, yet she had more sex appeal in her little finger than the rest of the bandbox-chic girls put together.

Ruark had also possessed that sex appeal, charisma, call it what you will, and in full measure. Set on course to charm, her ex-husband had been irresistible. Over the years a natural belligerence had distilled into sturdy confidence in himself, which Katrin had found magnetic. Ruark was his own man. He had no doubt that, despite the odds being stacked against him, he would eventually be successful. Outspoken and tough, he had swept into her life like a hurricane. She had never met anyone so incisive before. Her father, a placid individual to say the least, had paled in comparison, and the difference between her previous suitors and Ruark had been the difference between cheap wine and a deep rich claret. As if his cavalier attitude was not lethal enough, this one-hundred-and-eighty pounds of lean Australian beef came in at six foot two, with thick dark hair and astonishingly direct blue eyes. Eyes which, when he felt hostile, could be downright intimidating.

But why was she thinking about Ruark again? Katrin had good days and bad days. Good days when she almost believed herself to be the optimistic divorcée the world saw, and bad days when—bad days like today. Arlene was halfway along the catwalk before she suddenly emerged from her thoughts to realise she had said nothing.

'This afternoon dress of flowing chiffon would not disgrace a Buckingham Palace garden party,' Katrin recited hurriedly. 'Muted shades of bronze and vanilla predominate and the hemline, which hovers just below the knee, is flattering for any age-group. Add spindly high heels in vanilla

glacé leather, and this is an outfit which says
without any shade of doubt "I'm feminine".'

Arlene's resultant twitch of the hips brought a
smattering of applause. Katrin had reached the
end of her spiel and was silent, waiting for the
blonde to finish, when the arrival of a late diner
attracted her attention. A broad-shouldered man
in a pale beige suit was being led through the
tables, a waiter almost genuflecting before him.
The proud angle of the blue-black head, the
sheer vitality of his animal stride drew her eyes to
him. And other eyes, for his progress diverted
much attention from the catwalk. By the time he
sat down at a far table overlooking the palm trees
in the hotel gardens, the majority of females in
the restaurant had taken note. Katrin paled. Her
mind blew a fuse. Sparks flew inside her head. It
couldn't be! It *was*. Oh no! Her immediate
instinct was to flee, but another model had
arrived on the catwalk. Panic clogged her vocal
chords. She gulped, cleared her throat, found her
place.

'Roselind now, daring to dazzle in this
versatile hot pink blazer and skirt suit, perfect for
the office or a casual date.'

At the sound of her voice, the man's head jerked
up from the menu. He whipped off the
black-rimmed spectacles he had been using and
their eyes met. All Katrin's senses revved at full
throttle. In that instant she knew exactly why she
had fallen in love with him and why she had not yet
recovered from their divorce. Would she ever
recover? she wondered numbly, her eyes clinging
to his. Ruark had recovered. That much was
evident when he calmly replaced the spectacles and
returned to deciding what he would like to eat.

His detachment chilled, yet what else could she expect? Sitting there in style, the waiters hovering for his least command, Ruark looked like the kind of man who chatted daily with heads of state, and who had not the least intention of being knocked sideways by the sight of a mere woman, ex-wife or not. Katrin felt wretched. How did he come to be in Singapore? Why was he lunching at the Regent? A client must be joining him, he could never afford to eat here unless the company was footing the bill. For some obscure reason, she found herself praying the client would not turn out to be a woman, especially a young, good-looking woman.

The model girl on the ramp spun, unbuttoning the blazer to display a blouse of white satin, and Katrin heard herself dole out the description in amazingly serene tones. Now she knew what automatic pilot meant. You carried on functioning when, in reality, you were falling apart. Head swirling with a jumble of emotions, she had no idea how she reached the finale. Ruark never once bothered to acknowledge her presence again, yet ignoring him proved impossible. Katrin's gaze returned to him time after time, as if responding to a homing device. When the models grouped on the catwalk she gave a final plug for the boutique, advertised next week's show and added a quick mention of the Pivotelle Agency. There was a round of applause, though she saw Ruark did not participate, preferring instead to consult the wine list. The models, and some of the diners, melted away.

Katrin wondered what on earth to do. Did she take the coward's way out and melt away, too, pretending she had never seen him? Or maybe she was supposed to march over, clap him on the back and ask jovially, 'How's life, old boy?' If only there was a blueprint telling her how to behave. What was the social etiquette for divorced couples? Being civilised seemed important. Head must overrule heart. Folder and bag grasped firmly beneath her arm, she stepped down from the podium. If bizarre face twitches had developed in the time she took to reach Ruark's table, Katrin would not have been surprised, yet discovered on her arrival that she still possessed sufficient control to produce a bright smile.

'What a small world,' she said prosaically.

He rose to greet her, a black brow lifting. 'Isn't it? You're looking good, pussycat.'

His careless use of the pet name from the past hurt. She thought it sat oddly on the lips of this aloof stranger who was so much in control of the situation. But Ruark had always been in control.

'I won't intrude,' she said, determined to be nonchalant. 'I just thought I'd come across and say hello.'

'I should damn well think so,' he snapped, so unexpectedly incensed that her breath caught in her throat.

Maybe he wasn't aloof, maybe he wasn't in control? The moment the idea struck her, she wanted to laugh out loud at her foolishness. It had been Ruark's detachment which had attracted her in the first place. He had never fussed like her father, nor tried to domineer like Oliver. If only he had, she thought wistfully.

Ruark's anger was momentary, and he smiled. 'You're not intruding,' he assured her. 'I'm

eating alone. Will you join me? Can I order you
something?'

'No—no, thank you,' Katrin stammered.

His Italian blood meant Ruark's flashpoint
had always been easily reached. He was quick
to flare up, yet quick to forgive and forget. She
wondered why he had reacted so tetchily.
Normally his temper was reserved for things
he cared about, and he didn't care a toss about
her, *now*.

'You must have a glass of wine.'

She was given no opportunity to protest, for he
clicked his fingers to summon a waiter and in
seconds Katrin was installed beside him. She
struggled to find some conversation.

'How long have you been using those?' she
enquired, indicating the spectacles which lay on
the white damask cloth.

'A few weeks. Of late my eyes have been a little
. . . tricky.'

'How "tricky"?'

'Sore.'

'A throwback to your accident?'

He gave a noncommital shrug. 'Doubtful.
Probably it's the onset of old age.'

His tone told her he had no intention of
revealing more. Katrin well remembered his
distaste for talking about the dockside accident
which had happened before they met. In those
days Ruark had been a seaman, with a part share
in a cargo boat, along with his close companion,
Dick. The two men had grown up in the same
neighbourhood, attended the same schools, sailed
the world together. They had been close, very
close.

'Dick was my alter ego. The brother I never

had,' Ruark had told her once. 'When he died, it was as if something died in me.'

In addition to scarring him emotionally, the accident had left him with three physical scars. Katrin risked a glance at his brow where a silver line, as straight as if drawn by a ruler, travelled from the corner of his eye up into his hair. Crates of machinery tools had been in the process of being lifted in a rope net from the quay into the boat's hold, when a steel carrying cable had snapped. The crates had plummeted to the deck, and in a frantic bid to save Dick, Ruark had lunged forward. The broken cable had zigzagged, whiplashing through the air, unravelling wires at high speed and, intent on heaving the crates from his trapped friend, he had remained stubbornly in its path. A vicious strand of bare metal had raked his face, gouging out a bloody line of flesh and missing his eyes by the merest fraction, though the lids had been grazed. His shoulder took the brunt of a second whiplashing, his hip the third.

'Another inch closer, and I'd have been singing falsetto for the rest of my life,' he had joked, when Katrin had tenderly kissed the line which snaked across his thigh. But beneath his joking had been pain. After the accident, he had rejected the sea. 'Too much reminded me of Dick,' he had explained. 'I needed something different, without memories. I saw a job vacancy in advertising and decided to apply. This fool stepped in.' He had grinned, amused at the ease with which he had switched careers. 'Luckily I appear to be blessed with the necessary talents.'

Katrin forced herself to drink a mouthful of wine. 'Do you still keep in touch with Suzi?' she queried, surprised to discover her resentment at Ruark's close ties with Dick's widow was as strong as ever.

'Very much so. My flat in Sydney is close to where she lives, so I've been teaching her two boys to surf.'

'You have a flat in Sydney?'

When he nodded she flashed another bright smile, took another mouthful of red wine, and wondered what to say next. She was surprised he could afford to own a flat. But no doubt it was heavily mortgaged. Ruark must have bought the property as an investment, renting it out most of the time, and just taking possession himself for a few weeks each year when he flew back on holiday from Hong Kong. Katrin raised her head, having concocted a trite observation on the weather, but found she was being taken apart, inch by calculating inch. Her paper-thin composure tore a little more.

'You're thinner,' Ruark said.

'A pound or two.'

'And what's Felix's opinion of your leather gear?' he teased, mischief shining in his blue eyes.

'My father died close on a year ago.'

'Dear God! I'm sorry. I didn't know.' As if in reflex his hand shot across the table to cover hers for an instant, before he remembered their relationship and withdrew. 'He and I were poles apart, but Felix was a nice guy.'

'Yet no inner steel?'

A residue of bitterness filled her voice as she recalled an old quote, something Ruark had hissed during one of the stormy times. He had hissed so many impassioned words—living in the big house had meant there was no alternative but

to hiss, unless you wanted your quarrels
overheard by Uncle Tom Cobley and all—and
now, usually about four a.m. in the dead hours
of the night, every single word seemed to
resurrect itself. The volatile mixture of Italian
and Irish blood which flowed within him meant
Ruark's vocabulary was imaginative. Add his
years at sea, plus the forthrightness of
Australians, and he was articulate to the point
of brutality.

'Not much,' he agreed, and there was nothing
hypocritical or obtuse in his delivery.

'You haven't changed. You're still all heart,
aren't you?' Katrin demanded.

'You prefer me to tell lies?'

The arrival of a waiter bearing a platter of steak
tartare was a godsend. In the time the man took
to serve the food, Katrin managed to smooth her
ruffled feathers. Arguing with her ex-husband
five minutes after they'd met again was infantile.
Be civilised, she told herself. Be detached, like
Ruark.

'Are you in Singapore on business?' she asked,
as he began his meal.

'No. I came to see you. Though I never
realised, when a room was reserved for me here,
that Pivotelle would be responsible for the
fashion show.'

Her heart skipped a beat. 'Why do you want to
see me?'

'Because it's time we came to grips with the
past.'

'*I* have,' Katrin announced. 'If you haven't,
that's your funeral.'

Ruark paused, his fork halfway to his mouth,
and subjected her to one of his riveting, narrow-

eyed looks. 'Don't you ever wish we could begin again at the beginning?' he asked.

'It's a bit late for that,' she responded. Her stomach somersaulted madly. What was he saying? Did he mean he wanted them to start afresh? He couldn't—could he? A wave of totally disproportionate excitement threatened to swamp her. Katrin took a deep breath. 'Our marriage seems like it happened two lifetimes ago.'

'You've grown accustomed to being a free agent and you like it?' he suggested, attacking the steak tartare with gusto.

She hesitated, smiling uncertainly, then realised she would be a fool to admit how often she felt weak and miserable. 'Of course. There has to be more to life than constant battling, doesn't there?'

'Was our marriage constant battles? There were some very good times, and we also made pretty hot love. I remember how my toes used to curl up, and other parts of my anatomy.' He chuckled, manifestly masculine in his smugness, leaving her with flushed face and thoughts in turmoil. 'I presume you're still shacked up with Ollie?' he said abruptly.

'No. After Daddy died I moved into a small apartment near the Botanic Gardens,' she said, and saw his surprise.

'So Ollie's rattling around his sixteen rooms in splendid isolation?'

'He's been talking about selling the big house.'

Ruark laughed. 'He'll never do that. Ollie needs it as a constant reminder of how grand he is. His status symbols are vital to him—big old Colonial house, so many servants you trip over the damn things, monogrammed shirts which he has laundered daily by vestal virgins, the most underthumb stepsister in the whole of Singapore.'

'I see you still subscribe to the law which says you have to be a pain in the neck ninety per cent of the time,' Katrin said tightly. 'Oliver's been very kind. He was extremely supportive when my father had his stroke.'

She was all set to follow on with a glowing appraisal of her stepbrother's reliability, as diametrically opposed to Ruark's, when she noticed Arlene weaving through the tables towards them. Katrin knew she should be grateful for the interruption, but instead found her friend's arrival vaguely exasperating. Ruark, however, looked delighted. He and his fellow countrywoman had always hit it off, and as he rose to greet her, his smile was wide.

'Still the sexiest blonde on two legs,' he grinned.

Arlene hugged him and stood back, her eyes sliding up and down in open appraisal. 'And don't you look great! The affluent gent and how.' She fingered his lapel. 'How much did this little number cost?'

He winked. 'Enough. Come and join us.' Another click of his fingers and Arlene was also provided with wine.

'You always prophesied you'd hit the jackpot, and from the way you look today, I'd say you have,' the blonde surmised, laughing into his eyes. 'I wonder what took you so long?'

'I guess I was a late starter.'

'I guess you were.'

As the two of them began a teasing repartee, Katrin frowned. Throughout their marriage Ruark had owned only two suits, each one painstakingly cared for in order to impress his clients. He had always looked smart and respectable, but this expensive sheen was new.

'Are you and Katrin managing to behave like two adults?' Arlene asked him, bowling in where others might have feared to tread. She raised her glass. 'Good on you, mates.'

Katrin flashed Ruark a hasty glance, and saw a smile lurking in the corner of his mouth.

'My wife hasn't clasped me to her bosom, but neither has she kicked me in the teeth,' he grinned.

She was about to point out, very icily, that she was his *ex*-wife, but Arlene rushed in first.

'Why don't I rustle up some of the old gang from the tennis club and we can have a grand reunion? Everyone would love to see you again, Ruark. Will you be in town next weekend?'

He slid his spectacles back into their leather case and tucked them inside his breast pocket. 'I will. I expect to be here for as long as it takes.'

'Sorry, I'm busy next weekend,' Katrin interrupted, wondering what he could be referring to. Maybe he had some business deal on the brew, in addition to seeing her?

'Then how about the weekend after?' Arlene persisted, blind to Katrin's silent 'let me off the hook' message.

Doubtless getting them together was some kind of therapy in her friend's book, but it did not appeal one bit. If a simple drink in Ruark's company was doing such dreadful things to her composure, a full day with him was out of the question. She was civilised, but not *that* civilised.

'I don't think so,' Katrin said, but Arlene's attention had swung. She was back to fêteing

Ruark as if he was a hero, recently returned from the war.

'A week on Sunday sounds fine,' Ruark agreed, and the blonde's smile indicated the matter had now been settled to everyone's satisfaction.

'Do an old fan a favour?' Arlene placed her hand on his sleeve. 'Wear those short shorts of yours. I always did get itchy palms when I saw you dashing around the tennis court. You have the sexiest backside imaginable.'

He threw back his head and roared with laughter. 'I see feminism has hit South-East Asia at long last,' he chuckled. 'Okay, I'll do my best.'

After a few more minutes of their double act, Arlene looked at her watch. 'Must be off I'm afraid.'

Katrin hastily drained her glass. 'Yes, I must go, too.' She was so relieved at having survived the past quarter of an hour without any visible sign of panic, that she managed to give Ruark a wide smile. 'Perhaps I'll see you around?' she suggested glibly, vowing that the reunion would be vetoed, as far as she was concerned. Until she knew Ruark had left Singapore's shores, she would restrict her world solely to the model agency and her apartment. She had no intention of bumping into him by mistake.

'Wait a minute, Kat.' He gripped her wrist to detain her. There was no escape. With growing dismay Katrin watched Arlene make her goodbyes and walk off through the tables. 'Isn't it time we talked?' he questioned as he released her. Ruark lounged back in his chair, as though settling down to a long discussion.

'What is there to talk about?' she asked, hating herself for sounding so breathless.

The success of the fashion show had filled her
with a satisfying sense of personal esteem, yet in
Ruark's presence she seemed to have dwindled to
an insecure and useless female. Meeting his eyes
was impossible, so instead she fixed her gaze on
his hands, teak brown hands. His tan was twenty-
four carat, as always, she thought. Ruark adjusted
a cufflink, and when the shirt sleeve rode up
across his wrist, she caught a glimpse of his
tattoo. One of his seafaring friends had been a
Chinese cook. A devotee of the zodiac, Lim had
insisted that as Ruark had been born in the
desirous Year of the Dragon he should be marked
with the appropriate brand. Against his better
judgment and, so he said, because he was under
the influence of a beer too many, he had
succumbed. Now a dragon writhed in red, blue
and black, breathing fire at his damaged left
shoulder, with the tail's final curl at his wrist.

'Isn't it time we made a clean break?' he asked,
abandoning the cufflink.

'I thought we had.'

'A legal break, I mean.' His blue eyes pierced
hers. 'I want you to set me free. I want a divorce.'

CHAPTER TWO

KATRIN sat stern-faced. 'If this is your idea of a joke, I don't find it amusing.'

'Would I joke about such a thoroughly unpleasant situation?' he asked, and his voice took on a rasping edge, the Australian accent emphasised by his intensity. 'You must agree we can't stay in limbo forever. You have to face facts.'

'But we *are* divorced!'

'Talk sense!'

'I am.'

'When, where, how?' he quizzed, blatantly disbelieving her.

'Almost a year ago. The papers were sent to you.'

'I've received nothing. Dear God, you can't divorce someone without them knowing a blind thing about it!'

'Well, I did. I have.' Katrin's heart began to pound wildly against her breastbone. 'You must have given your permission and later received the decrees. You *must*. The documents would have been forwarded to your company address in Hong Kong. By registered post, I imagine.'

'I was only in Hong Kong for a short time before being transferred to the States. And for the past six months or so, I've been based in Australia.'

'So you actually live in Sydney full time?'

The discovery that he hadn't been where she

had placed him in her mind's eye was un-reasonably irritating. She had been deceived. With one sentence he had nullified days, weeks, months of her carefully constructed imaginings.

'Yes. I have a flat, like I said. But my change of locations doesn't make any difference. All my mail was forwarded on. Nothing has gone astray.'

'The divorce papers obviously have!'

The tip of his tongue sneaked out to touch the corner of his mouth, a habit she remembered from previous moments of high tension.

'There must be crossed wires somewhere,' Ruark decided. 'Start at the beginning and tell me exactly what happened.'

Katrin did not have much stomach for reliving the traumas of the past, not when she had presumed they were all safely behind her, but he was waiting for a reply. Because there seemed no alternative, she plunged headlong into a recital.

'Once it became obvious that things weren't going to—to alter between us I saw a solicitor, a Mr Beng, and he acted on my behalf. I went to his office, and he made me go through the story of our marriage. He took notes. He said that as the relationship appeared to have——' She heard her voice crack. '—To have broken down irretrievably, everything would be straight-forward. He agreed to set the legal wheels in motion.'

'He knew we'd been married barely a year?'

'Yes.'

'And yet there was no suggestion we might try again? That we get in touch and be reconciled?'

'None,' she said helplessly. How could he be so rational? Ruark sounded as if he was discussing another couple, totally separate from them. 'Mr

Beng prepared the documents, and—and he charged the earth.'

'The court granted a divorce?'

'*Yes*. You never came back.' She searched his eyes desperately. 'You never——'

'I wrote.'

Katrin recalled a postcard promising he'd be in touch later, but the promise had never been fulfilled. 'Oh, that!'

'Yes, that. Look, I'm trying to stay calm here, but I'd like to state forcibly how very much I object to being tossed on to the slagheap when you don't even have the courtesy to consult me.'

'You didn't want a divorce?' she asked tremulously.

'Not one no-one bothers to tell me about.' He raked an agitated hand through his thick black hair. 'You imbecile, how could you do this to me? I was one half of our partnership. I was your husband.'

Katrin gave a sour little laugh. 'Ruark, you were never my husband. A playmate, a lover, the guy who shared occasional meals with me, and who read poetry at midnight, but a husband, no!'

'It's fair to point out that you were never much of a wife, either,' he retorted, determined he would not be burdened with all the blame. 'You speak of shared meals, but you never cooked them. In the year we were together you didn't once make me so much as a sandwich. You never washed any of my clothes or——'

'Did you want me to spend my time cooking and washing?' she demanded.

'I wanted you to look after me. Okay, maybe washing my socks sounds an odd thing to wish for, but at least it would have been proof that you were something more than—than my mistress!'

'But I didn't have any opportunity to——'

'Opportunity?' he blazed. 'What opportunity did I have to be a husband with you emotionally fastened to your father, and damned Ollie breathing down my neck? Dear God, he was an arch-critic if there ever was one.' Ruark gave a harsh grunt of remembrance. 'But I had the last laugh. Oliver may have possessed the wealth and the power, but I possessed you. I derived a distinct thrill from us lying naked in bed together, knowing he was down the hallway in his room and must be aware of what was happening. I hoped he heard when you cried out at the moment of climax, a climax *I'd* brought you to.'

'That's obscene.'

'That's natural.' Ruark rubbed his fingers slowly up and down the stem of his wineglass. 'So, what kind of divorce package was cooked up?' he drawled. 'Doubtless dear Ollie gave you the benefit of his advice?'

'He recommended Mr Beng,' she agreed stiffly. 'But he didn't interfere.' Ruark arched his brows in exaggerated surprise. 'Well, he did keep track of the proceedings while Daddy was in hospital,' she confessed, wishing vehemently things could have been different. 'He was trying to make life easier for me.'

'How kind! I bet he shouted hip-hip-hooray from the rooftops at the chance of ridding you of me. I'm only surprised he didn't attempt to latch on to the meagre resources I had available at the time. Or did he?' His eyes glittered like those of a dangerous animal about to advance. 'Are you now about to drop another bombshell and announce

that in addition to this somewhat doubtful
divorce, there's a year's alimony to be settled?
I'm not about to be dragged off to jail for non-
payment of maintenance, am I?'

'I never claimed a penny,' Katrin replied,
choking on a lump of bewildered misery. 'And
our divorce isn't doubtful.' Sitting here in public
arguing with him was impossible, she could not
bear it a moment longer. The naked aggression
he was displaying was natural, Ruark must be in
a state of shock, but she was also in shock at
seeing him so unexpectedly. 'I must go. I have to
take a deportment class back at Pivotelle in thirty
minutes, and——' She glanced wildly around the
restaurant. 'We seem to be the only people left
here.'

'Ring the agency and find someone else to
take the class,' he instructed, as he signed the
bill. 'I'm sorry, but I can't accept that we're
divorced. How can it be for real if I didn't give
my permission? I don't know much about the
mechanics of such things, let alone here in
Singapore, but surely I should have been given
the opportunity to say yeah or nay?' He
narrowed his eyes. 'Are you sure the divorce is
genuine?'

'Of course I'm sure,' she replied pettishly.

'Okay, but I want you to take me through the
entire process, one step at a time. You owe me
that.' He rose. 'We'll go up to my room, we won't
be disturbed there.'

Katrin rushed ahead, swivelling when they
reached the lobby. 'No. I can't, I can't,' she
cried.

'Can't what? Bring yourself to explain what's
happened? Or be alone in a bedroom with me?'

His grin was wicked. 'Are you frightened that after a gap of fifteen months or so those wayward hormones of yours might tempt you to rip the clothes off me and gobble me up?'

'My hormones are not wayward.'

'They used to be. I can remember a tender young virgin begging me to take advantage of her. And didn't she stamp her foot when I insisted we wait until we were married?'

Katrin cringed at this embarrassing reminder of her immaturity and became very industrious, searching for the car valet ticket. 'I can't avoid taking the deportment class, Ruark, and there are other matters which require my attention at Pivotelle. I'm quite willing to explain what's happened, but later.'

'This evening?'

Her mind resembled a volcano, spilling questions and red-hot emotions on all sides. Time was desperately needed in which to pull herself together again. Seeing him this evening was much too soon.

She flashed a paste smile. 'Sorry, I'm busy this evening.'

'When can you fit me in?' he demanded. 'Hell, I fly over here and find I'm to be treated like a damned leper. I consider I deserve a prompt explanation of what you've been doing to *my* life, don't you?'

'Yes, yes, I suppose so. Come to the agency tomorrow, around eleven-thirty,' she offered, feeling like a tent peg Ruark was intent on hammering into the ground. 'I'll be finished with the poise and personality class by then.' The irony of her presuming to instruct others on poise of all things, made her want to shriek with manical laughter, but instead Katrin gave an indeterminate nod. 'That be okay?'

Ruark touched a makebelieve forelock. 'Yes, ma'am. As you say, ma'am.' His wry humour vanished, to be replaced by that shrewd, almost insolent, stare which she knew so well. 'But I need to know something now, to be going on with. Did you motivate this divorce yourself, or did Ollie put you up to it?'

Her violet eyes flashed. 'Do you think I'd allow someone else to make a decision like that?'

'I don't know,' he said after a moment. 'I honestly don't know.'

'Then you don't know the real me.' Katrin was tart.

He moved his broad shoulders. 'Maybe not.'

'Goodbye then.' She turned to go.

'You've forgotten something.'

She looked at him. 'What?'

'This.'

He slid an arm around her shoulders and pulled her against him, his mouth coming down on hers so positively that Katrin had no time to resist.

She slept badly that night. In recent weeks she had almost persuaded herself she was capable of rebuilding a satisfactory life without Ruark, but now her future had collapsed like a house of cards. One thing was horribly clear; her reaction towards him had been strong, too strong. Without knowing why, she had responded to his kiss, and only when the tip of his tongue had probed her lips had common sense returned and she had jerked away. Throughout the silent hours of the night her feelings shot up and down, like shadows on a wall. What she felt for Ruark could not be love—how could you still love a man who had dumped an ultimatum on your lap and walked out so callously?—yet his attraction continued to be lethal.

Morning came at last, and Katrin crawled out of bed to inspect the reflection in the mirror. Beneath her tan she was pale, ghostly shadows circling her eyes, yet she knew a skilful application of make-up would cancel the wan look. If only she could cancel out the wan feeling which existed inside her so competently! But the prospect of another head-on meeting with Ruark already had her on edge. She hated her emotions being put through the wringer like this, and she hated recalling the divorce. All of a sudden her self-confidence seemed to have shrivelled to the size of a sultana. Katrin bit deep into her lip. Even if some fluke meant Ruark had not given his permission, everything was legal wasn't it? Yes, it had to be. Mr Beng had never mentioned any snags, and Oliver had praised the solicitor as being sharpwitted and shrewd.

'Benny Beng is a member of my Rotary Club,' her stepbrother had said, by way of a testimonial. 'An upright and affluent one at that.'

Katrin pulled back her shoulders and recognised her wild imaginings for what they were—a peculiarly feminine form of hysteria.

Yesterday her outfit had been jaunty, but today she would be the epitome of elegance. A sought-after model, she continued to go before the camera whenever some particularly juicy assignment occurred, and excelled in creating different images. Katrin had no illusions. She was not beautiful—not compared to Lisu or some of the other models—but her versatility was tremendous. She could project pert coyness, be wide-eyed and daisy-fresh, or play the dignified high-society lady at will; a change of costume and cosmetics, and a certain inward posturing was all she required. So why couldn't she project a cool image when she met Ruark? Today she would, Katrin decided. Today she would be detached. Today she would show him how she had developed, that the somewhat pampered girl had crystallised into a mature woman.

Her soft silk chiffon dress was in sunset stripes of honey, orange and papaya, girdled with a narrow tan suede belt. Her heels were high, her face meticulously painted. First on the agenda was a call at the bank, where the manager received her with due ceremony, so the time was approaching ten o'clock when she entered the premises of the Pivotelle Model Agency. The suite was compact—reception area, her office, and a general studio where the classes took place, but everything was neat. The walls were cream, the carpet coffee, and there were lashings of healthy green pot plants. Colourful blow-ups of magazine covers and advertisements which had featured Pivotelle models were prominently displayed.

Michelle, the receptionist, reported several matters requiring attention, so Katrin dealt with them before opening the post. She was pleased to find an enquiry from a major department store, and also one from a perfumery. Both were planning promotions later in the year and needed Pivotelle's services. The agency's continuing success was obvious, which served to harden her resolve—she would not enter any models for the

DeSouza competition. There was no reason why she must bend to Oliver's whims. What convinced him he was an expert on the modelling world when he spoke from a position of complete ignorance, she did not know. But her stepbrother was convinced of his expertise on most things, Katrin thought with wry amusement. Once she had rarely protested, believing him to know best whatever the circumstances, but she had grown up. The days of unquestioning obedience were dead and gone. Like her father. Like her marriage.

After she had read the mail, she locked it away in the cabinet and pocketed the key. Oliver did not leave for Antwerp until the next day and had developed a habit of arriving at Pivotelle unannounced. She suspected that if she didn't happen to be in the room, whatever lay on her desk was inspected as a matter of course. Oliver would justify his action as being 'family', but as far as Katrin was concerned he was a busybody, prying into matters which did not concern him.

'That's all for now, girls,' she said, when the clock on the studio wall reached eleven-thirty. 'This week please practise how to climb in and out of cars gracefully, and do remember the correct way to sit. You aren't rag dolls with knees lolling apart, you're respectable young ladies.' She beckoned to a student in a black leotard. 'Your mother phoned, Lisu, to ask if you could be included in a fashion show fairly soon,' she explained when the girl came over. 'I'd like to check whether you yourself feel confident enough?'

Lisu studied her shoes. 'Mother would be

thrilled if I had the chance to appear at the Regent. She considers the hotel has status.'

'And would *you* be thrilled?' Katrin probed.

'I managed those two photographic sessions last week, didn't I?' The liquid-coal eyes which met hers were pleading.

'You did, but managing isn't enough,' she pointed out gently. 'If you climb on to a catwalk and every step is an ordeal, your misery transmits itself to the audience. Being a model should be fun—fun for you, and everyone else.'

'My mother says I'll enjoy modelling once I learn to hang loose.'

Katrin almost choked. With Mrs Ho in the background to prod and poke, there was a minimal chance of poor Lisu ever hanging loose. Still, she supposed there was a certain wisdom in allowing the girl a practice run. If she didn't, the despotic Mrs Ho would be sure to increase the pressure and make life difficult for both her and Lisu. And then there was always the slim hope that the girl, herself, would realise she was no natural-born model, and rebel.

'Would you like to be included in one of the lunchtime shows?' Katrin asked.

'Mummy would be delighted.'

'But would you?' she asked, trying hard to prise out a commitment.

Lisu's fingers had become twisted into a cat's cradle.

'I'd prefer the hair show,' she confessed. 'That requires only a single walk on stage, doesn't it?'

'One by yourself, plus the collective finale. I suppose it would be the lesser of the two evils,' Katrin agreed. 'A little bit of footwork might need to be memorised, but I could ask the choreographer to keep things simple in your case.'

'I'll do the hair show then, please.' Lisu sounded relieved and grateful.

'A rehearsal is scheduled for the afternoon of the show,' she explained. 'Michelle will confirm the time once everything has been finalised.'

'I've given Michelle my new photographs,' the girl said, following Katrin into the reception area. She pointed to a large brown envelope on the desk. 'There they are.'

'New ones?' Her brow creased. 'But you had a batch taken only a couple of months ago, and they were fine.'

'My mother decided they could be improved upon.'

'Bully for mum,' Katrin muttered, promising to look through the new collection later that day.

'Mr Lencioni's waiting in your office,' Michelle announced, brimming with curiosity at this sudden reappearance of her employer's ex-husband. 'I've taken him in some tea.'

'Thanks.' Katrin's mask of cool efficiency was firmly in place. 'Were there any phone calls while I was taking the class?'

'Three,' her receptionist said, disappointed by such a matter-of-fact response.

'And they were?'

Cursing this need for delaying tactics, Katrin spoke to each caller in turn. Her stomach churned with increasing fervour and she wondered whether it was natural to feel so uptight about meeting her ex-husband again. *Ex*-husband—the 'ex' seemed to clatter like a dustbin lid around her head. But a divorce was only a means of righting a wrong, of correcting a mistake, so why was she weighed down by a barrage of guilt? She had done nothing to be ashamed of, she had nothing to fear. When the third call ended, no more reasons not to join Ruark could be found.

'Good morning.' She strode briskly into her office. 'I hope I've not kept you waiting too long?'

He was at the window behind her desk, fingers bending down a slat of the venetian blind to give access to a view of the sunlit street. He turned, and the blind snapped back into place.

'I didn't flatter myself you'd drop everything the moment I arrived,' he commented, and walked round the desk to dump himself in a chair.

Casually dressed this morning, he was wearing jeans and a blue-and-white striped shirt. Casual but costly, Katrin found herself assessing. The jeans were a long way from the ten-dollar variety he used to haggle over so successfully in the cubicle shops of Change Alley.

'I have a business to run,' she reminded him stiffly.

'The hotshot career woman. So independent that all she needs is Ollie providing a safety net every inch of the way.'

Her cheeks grew pink. 'That's not true!'

Ruark leant forward, hands jammed between his knees. 'Where is it?' he demanded.

Katrin was bemused. 'Where's what?'

'The decree absolute. I presume there's a piece of paper which tells the world how you've gone your way and I've gone mine?' He raised his dark head and sardonically scanned the office. 'Maybe Ollie has had the decree framed in gold? To be displayed as proof positive that the Aussie bastard's been cut adrift?'

She ignored his sarcasm. 'I didn't realise you'd want to see the decree.'

'Naturally. And I'll need copies. I presume you were first granted a decree nisi, then six weeks later the decree absolute followed?' She nodded. 'I'd like copies of both please. Plus my own certificates, or whatever paperwork discarded husbands receive on these occasions.'

Without warning the reason behind his request hit her as forcibly as a knee in her stomach. 'You're—you're going to be married again?' Katrin gasped, and when he shrugged acceptance her thoughts began tumbling over themselves like clothes in a washing machine. Too late she admitted to a mental block where Ruark's motives for his return were concerned. But now everything made sense. He was too sociable a man to derive satisfaction from living alone, and too virile to be satisfied with sleeping alone! A second wife was a foregone conclusion. She quaked, demoralised by the idea of being superseded by a Mark Two Mrs Lencioni. What kind of woman was lined up to take her place in his arms and in his bed? Some pint-sized blonde like Suzi, Dick's widow?

Ruark tapped his fingers on the desk to secure her attention.

'I need to have a look at both decrees,' he told her.

She picked herself up. 'I'll find them.'

'Find? Don't you know where they are?'

'Not exactly.'

'Shouldn't such important documents be kept under lock and key?' he suggested, trapping her glance.

'I suppose so, but what with my father dying and me moving from the big house everything's been . . . muddled,' she hedged.

'But you have a good idea where to locate them?'

'They're somewhere among a whole jumble of files I have at home. I was intending to look through them sometime, but—well, I've been busy.'

'You have seen the decrees?' His narrowed gaze and rigid shoulders reminded her of an interrogator who would not stop asking questions until she cracked.

'Not actually.' The violet eyes which had been locked with his swerved away.

'What!'

'There wasn't any need.' How could she explain that she had never been able to summon up the enthusiasm to search among the files? That she had not had the courage to read the facts in stark black and white? Katrin resolved her dilemma imperfectly. 'I know they're there, so I didn't bother.'

'You didn't bother! If you've never set eyes on the papers how the hell can you be sure the divorce went through?' Ruark demanded, glaring as if he'd willingly tie her to a stake and be ready with the first match.

'Because I've seen Mr Beng's account. Oliver showed it to me. All the various stages of the divorce are given in detail, and there's a list of documents which came from the court. Mr Beng received both decrees and forwarded——'

'Why did Oliver have the account?' he cut in. 'Don't tell me. He paid it—right? Your stepbrother paid for our divorce,' he asserted, his anger giving each word a metallic resonance.

Katrin's cheeks burnt. 'Initially yes, but——'

He raised a hand. 'Save me the waffle.'

'I'm not waffling,' she protested, knowing that every word she uttered came out wrong and weak and puerile. She had so much wanted Ruark to realise how she had changed, how capable she was of running her own life, but instead she seemed to be proving exactly the opposite. 'My father's stroke occurred slap-bang in the middle of the divorce going through, and Oliver paid the account without consulting me.'

Ruark's lip curled. 'Because he's family?'

'Because he intended to be helpful.'

'Huh!'

'All right, interpret the situation your own way, but if you dare to tell me I've no inner steel I shall take the greatest pleasure in kicking you in the——'

'In the what?' he asked when she paused.

'In the backside,' she said, her smile daggers-drawn.

To her surprise, Ruark grinned. He leant back in his chair, one ankle held loosely at his knee by two tanned hands. 'You have inner steel, pussycat. Do you think I'd have married you otherwise? You also have your faults, but by and large you're a pretty gutsy lady. As I know to my cost.'

Was he giving her a bouquet or a brickbat? Katrin could not decide, but his blue eyes were so affable that she was tempted to grin back at him. She didn't. She remembered how she was supposed to be detached.

'I'll find both decrees this evening,' she promised.

'Want me to come along and help?'

'No, thank you.' Her reply had been too quick, too defensive, Ruark's glance told her so. But she didn't need his company, not when he still possessed the capacity to spin her heart out of control. Her heart, and her emotions, needed to be rock steady if she was to cope with this situation like a sensible, civilised human being. 'I'll drop the papers off at the Regent tomorrow morning on my way to work,' she suggested.

Ruark rose to his feet. 'Bring them up to my room,' he said, his voice slow and silky. 'Play your cards right, pussycat, and you might even earn yourself a good-morning kiss.'

Remembering the touch of his lips and the sudden need which had stampeded through her veins yesterday, Katrin frowned. 'I'll leave an envelope at the reception desk,' she told him.

'Coward.' He reached the doorway and turned, a tall bronzed figure with laughing eyes. 'How about you and me having one last glorious tumble in the hay?' He grinned at her, the corner of his mouth lifting in amused query. 'For old times' sake?'

Reflex clenched her hands into fists. What hope had she of laying the ghost of their love when Ruark spoke like this? How could he be so careless, so easy? Katrin attempted to answer in the same light way, but knew she didn't quite make it.

'Why not? When it's haymaking time I'll give you a call.'

'But not before?'

'No.'

'And if my memory serves me correct, Singapore always has been fresh out of autumns?'

he asked, and she nodded mutely. 'Which means, no tropical haymaking?' She nodded again. 'Pity,' he said, and left.

CHAPTER THREE

TUGGING the tea chest from the broom cupboard, along the hall and into the living room was hard work. Katrin straightened, panting a little, and mopped a film of sweat from her brow. If she had had any sense she would have closed the glass doors to the balcony and turned the air conditioner on to 'high cool', but just now sensible thought was elusive. Instead the doors were open wide, and she guessed the temperature must be in the eighties, despite it being mid-evening and the sun having set long ago.

A glass of iced lime juice in her hand, she walked out on to the balcony to take a break. Her seventh-floor apartment overlooked the Botanic Gardens on the rim of the city, and in spreading banyan trees below she heard the high-pitched drone of cicadas. The Gardens had been one of her and Ruark's favourite haunts—the Gardens and the beaches. Singapore was fringed with idyllic shores, and moonlight's silvery touch had made them even more magical. Or had Ruark been responsible for the magic? His courtship of her had been whirlwind, but low-key. Of necessity their pleasures had come free of charge, by courtesy of nature.

'That sailor of yours must be on a very low rung,' Oliver had commented, noting the singular lack of visits to expensive night spots. 'But then, of course, he never went to university *and* he changed careers midstream.'

'So?' Katrin had challenged.

'So he won't be able to afford to keep you in the manner to which you're accustomed.'

She had tossed her head. 'That doesn't bother me.'

It didn't. To be holding hands with Ruark on some silvery shore was paradise enough. Other young men had driven to her door in swanky sports cars, loaded her down with chocolates and presents, then proceeded to bore her stiff. Not so Ruark. Every minute with him was exciting, stimulating, wonderful. He never ceased to surprise her. On the surface he appeared ruthless and tough—when he played sports, winning was all—yet he possessed a deeply sensitive streak. Lines of poetry could enchant him, Beethoven's symphonies had him spellbound, and when he had first told her he loved her and had given her a single red rosebud, now pressed between the pages of a book of sonnets, his voice had trembled with emotion.

Katrin sipped the lime juice. Had this apartment attracted her because of the position, overlooking as it did the paths where they had so often strolled together hand in hand? No, she was manufacturing motives. Memories had not influenced her decision to live here. What had appealed was the reasonable rent, the modern kitchen, the easily managed lay-out which meant an amah was not necessary. Prior to the move she had been nervous because she had no experience of housework, but had soon discovered the satisfaction in tending her own little nest. Not that one person on their own made much work. Each week she whizzed through the rooms, polishing and vacuuming, but more for her own satisfaction than to remedy any dust layer or untidiness.

How different everything had been when Ruark was around. Sailors were reputed to like things shipshape and Bristol fashion, but her husband had been the exception. He habitually left heaps of loose change all over the place, could never find his briefcase, marked a path to the shower with crumpled shirts and kicked-off shoes. And the bed! Katrin had often wondered what the servants had thought about the screw of the sheets, the pillows on the floor. Perhaps, like Oliver, the servants had overheard them making love? She squirmed, thinking how *noisy* they must have been, her especially. But they had come straight from their honeymoon to the big house, living cheek by jowl with her father—once again a widower—Oliver, and the platoons of paid help. Their rapturous lovemaking had been the lovemaking of two young healthy animals. What else did anyone expect?

The papers which crammed the tea chest had been pushed in at random on the day she had moved, so sorting through took time. She found files on insurance, files dealing with income tax, files relating to her five years at an English boarding school. Her father appeared to have retained every single sheet of correspondence he had ever received, and in date order. When the tea chest was empty, Katrin sat crosslegged on the floor and sighed. Any papers she had needed to keep in the past had habitually been slipped into her father's filing system. Oliver knew that, so, being a creature of logic, he would have included the decrees when they had appeared. She screwed up her face, trying to recall the hazy days of her father's illness and the divorce. Had Oliver ever mentioned the decrees and told her what he had done with them? At the time, her stepbrother had dealt with all the post. She had been either occupied at the hospital, or trying to catch up on lost sleep. Reading the day's letters had seemed unimportant. But surely Oliver would have commented on the receipt of something so vital? Maybe he had, or maybe he had just filed them away, not wishing to upset her further at such a bad time?

The folders marked 'Personal' and 'Miscellaneous' had already been searched, but now she dismantled each individual file in turn. She didn't finish until after midnight. Katrin pushed the dark hair from her brow with dusty fingers and sighed again. Not a single scrap of paper in the tea chest related to her divorce.

'Then where the hell are the decrees?' Ruark demanded, when she telephoned him the following morning.

'At the big house.'

'With Oliver?' he sneered, disgust rife.

'Must be.' His reaction scraped across her frazzled nerves, and Katrin answered defensively. 'The sequence of events is difficult to remember because at the time I was worried sick about my father, but I expect Oliver——'

'Took charge?' he inserted before she could finish.

'More or less,' she had to admit.

There was a grunt which said, 'Just what I expected,' then Ruark snapped, 'Do you head for Ollie's mausoleum and collect or do I?'

'I'll go,' she said hurriedly.

'When? I didn't come to Singapore to be kept dangling on a string. I want action.'

'You always did,' she retorted. 'But I'd rather not involve Oliver, if possible. He flies to Antwerp this afternoon, so I'll time my visit when I know he's left for the airport. I'll drop the decrees round to you at the Regent as soon as I can.'

'Be snappy,' he ordered.

Katrin scowled at the telephone. 'Don't fret. You'll soon be able to scuttle back to your lady love, paperwork clutched in your hot little hand.' She paused, and a masochistic urge prompted her to ask the question which had been scratching at her mind since the previous day. 'Are you marrying Suzi?'

'Dear God, no! Whatever made you think that?'

'Because you and she were always . . . friends,' she said lamely.

'And still are. No, next time my bride is to be a big butch Sheila, one who spends her time throwing rocks at wallabies. Get a move on, finding those decrees. See you.'

He broke the connection before she had a chance to say anything else, and Katrin jammed her lips together in fury. His abrupt cut-off rankled. By contrast to how she felt right now, the intervening months without him took on retrospective serenity, though perhaps it had been the serenity of the benumbed. But she would survive, she told herself. Once Ruark left Singapore she would start life afresh. She would accept dates from all-comers and throw herself into the social scene like a creature possessed. Didn't broken bones heal to become stronger than unbroken ones?

Much to her relief, Ruark did not eat lunch in the Regent's restaurant that day, and when the fashion show ended Katrin pointed her car north. Oliver's house was on a discreetly expensive lane which backed against the lush amphitheatre of the race course. Displayed like a white-stuccoed jewel on green velvet lawns, the vast house, with its billiard room and minstrel gallery, was more suited to the days of the Raj. For months Katrin had avoided a visit, and returning brought the difference between her past lifestyle and how she now lived into sharp focus. Her apartment was one of many in a bustling block occupied by young Singaporeans, who waved cheery hellos and rushed around at a hectic pace. Here the only person she saw as she drove along the lane was a gardener, languidly sweeping up hibiscus blossoms. Doubtless servants ironed clothes in laundry rooms and solitary 'mems' catnapped prior to the driver ferrying them out for an afternoon bridge game, but this suspended animation was a far cry from what Katrin considered to be 'real life'.

She rang the bell, and had to wait several minutes before an old Chinese woman in a grey tunic and baggy black trousers opened the door.

'Hello, Missy,' she grinned, blinking her surprise. 'Good to see you after all this time. You look very smart.'

'Thanks, Ah Lan.' Having driven straight over from the fashion show, Katrin was wearing a white trouser suit and strapless gold lurex top. 'I hope I haven't disturbed your siesta?'

'Me happy wake up, see you,' the amah assured her, and led the way into the parquet-floored drawing room. 'You come call on Tuan Oliver? He no here.'

'No, I don't want to see him. I've come to collect some papers, that's all,' she explained. 'How's the family? Did your granddaughter have a girl or a boy? I've been longing to know but Tuan Oliver couldn't tell me.'

'A boy, a big, big boy,' the proud grandmother said, and set off into a voluble account of what was happening to the various members of her large family. 'Why you no come back live here?' she questioned, when Katrin had been brought up to date. 'I like talk you. Tuan Oliver no talk. He say me yap-yap-yap.' Ah Lan chuckled, demonstrating with her fingers. 'But I say he dab-dab-dab.'

'The buttons on his calculator?' Katrin guessed.

The amah nodded. 'Mealtimes, no talk just dab-dab. Not like when you here.'

Katrin gave an embarrassed smile. She knew how remote Oliver could be with the servants and felt annoyed. He treated Ah Lan and the others in a very lordly way, never showing the slightest interest in their lives.

'But surely the work is easier when you have only one Tuan to look after?' she suggested encouragingly.

Ah Lan's downward turn of mouth rejected the idea. 'Spirits no like this house now. Tuan Ruark go, your Daddy die, now you gone. Bad joss.'

'Never mind. Perhaps Tuan Oliver will come home with a bride one day and produce lots of children,' Katrin said, grinning. 'Maybe six or seven, all boys,' she added, knowing Ah Lan's predilection for male children.

'Pooh! He no do that. He no like children. All he like is dab-dab.' The old woman folded her arms and smiled. 'Now Tuan Ruark, he different.'

'I think the papers I'm looking for will be in the gloryhole,' Katrin inserted, unwilling to listen to Ah Lan's memories of Ruark. They were certain to be fond. Her husband, with his inbuilt democracy, had been an instant hit. Ruark had wandered into the kitchen, spent hours mending Ah Lan's son's motorbike, talked, listened and laughed with all the members of the amah's family. It had never occurred to him not to treat them as equals, and they had responded accordingly.

'Okay, missy. You go look.' Ah Lan patted away a yawn. 'I go back shut-eye. You give me shout when you leave.'

'I will,' she promised, as the amah shuffled off to the kitchen and her quarters beyond.

Katrin collected the key to the gloryhole, which was hidden as usual beneath a grotesque Japanese vase, and walked through to the hall. The gloryhole, or lazaretto as Ruark had nautically insisted, was a large cupboard beneath the staircase. In most households the flotsam and jetsam would have been pushed in to moulder, but this was Oliver's domain. When she unlocked the door and switched on the light, a glance showed that everything was immaculate. Rows of shelves, obviously dusted down on a regular basis, held a miscellany of items, and two gleaming filing cabinets stood side by side against the back wall. Like her father Oliver was methodical, and a quick check of headings in both cabinets revealed that what lay within related purely to financial matters. Her step-brother might not be interested in his servants, but he was interested in money. The dab-dab Ah Lan had spoken of referred to his fascination with squeezing extra cents out of his investments. Katrin let out a sigh of frustration. There was a wealth of information on treasury bonds and share transactions, but where had Oliver secreted the divorce papers? The prospect of asking him to release what, after all, was *her* property was unpalatable. She would be forced to explain that Ruark had arrived on the island, and she knew all the old lectures and criticisms would begin again.

'As your stepbrother, I feel I'm entitled to point out,' she could imagine him saying.

Katrin raised her eyes to the topmost shelf and started to scan slowly back and forth, working her way down. There were boxes of golf balls and cricket pads, an old radio, photograph albums, several pairs of shoes which Oliver could not bear to throw away. Only when she reached floor level did she notice a flat cardboard box bound with sticky tape, which had been pushed behind a torn badminton net. 'Beng—solicitor's letters etc.' Oliver had printed across the top in felt tip pen. Relief flooded through her.

'At last,' she breathed.

Back home, she had barely replaced the receiver after checking with Michelle that there were no problems at the agency, when the phone rang.

'Got them?' Ruark asked, with no preamble.

'Almost.'

'Almost? What's the delay this time? Anyone would imagine you had some hang-up about proving we're divorced. This reluctance to show me the decrees is downright Freudian. You're not having second thoughts, are you?'

'No, I'm damn well not!' Katrin threw back. 'I've collected a box containing the relevant papers from Oliver's and I'm just about to open it.'

'I'll be right over,' he said.

A man in a constant hurry, she thought, frowning at the lifeless telephone in her hand. Presumably he had the address from the phone book. Ruark had allowed no time for her to protest that he need not come, that she would deliver the decrees to him. She did not want him on *her* territory. A meeting at the Regent would have been far more suitable. The apartment held no memories of him, and she had hoped to keep it that way. But now Ruark would sprawl on the mango-and-white-flowered sofa, comment on the view, and she knew every word, every movement, would be stored up in her mind to be dissected at a later date.

Katrin pounced on the box, tearing a lacquered nail in her haste to rip off the crisscrossing strips of tape. If the decrees could be located quickly, maybe she could hand them over to Ruark at the door? But the tape was as tight as bindings on an Egyptian mummy. No sooner did she manage to pick one end free, than another obstinate strip defied every attempt to shift it. She was in the kitchen, frantically searching for scissors, when the doorbell rang.

'What did you come by—jet plane?' she enquired, as Ruark followed her into the living room.

'No. I had a taxi driver who handled his cab like Starsky, or is it Hutch? Anyhow, at one point we seemed destined for the morgue, but——' He spread two hands. 'Here I am.'

'So I see.'

Katrin peeled off her white jacket and flung it on to the sofa. The futile attack on the box had already raised her temperature, and now Ruark's too-prompt arrival was raising it even further. He looked cool and relaxed in navy shirt and trousers, while she was hotly flustered. In irritation she plucked away a dark strand of hair which was sticking to her forehead.

'Would you like a knife to slit my throat?' he asked, pushing both hands into his trouser pockets and grinning.

'I'm sorry.' Beneath the amused beam of his blue eyes, her anger collapsed. 'It's just that at first I couldn't find the papers at the big house, and now I can't open the box. I've broken a fingernail and——' She threw him a quick glance. 'And to be honest, being with you again after all this time is something of a traumatic occasion.'

'That works both ways, pussycat.'

'It does?'

He smiled at her surprise. 'I realise it's supposed to be stiff upper lip for me, but I feel, too. Do you think I haven't gone through hell, wondering whether leaving for Hong Kong was the right thing to do? So many times I've been tempted to pick up the phone and talk.'

'Why didn't you?' she asked, wishing he wouldn't play hide and seek with her emotions like this. Their marriage had broken up long ago, what was the point in this backtracking?

'Because I resented having to give my name to a servant, who would then broadcast the information to the entire household. Foolish, I know, but there you are.' Ruark shrugged away the feeling and laughed. 'I must have used up a whole tree writing letters, most of which ended their days in the wastepaper basket.'

'You don't write letters.'

'Don't I?' He put out his hand and rubbed the tip of his index finger slowly back and forth across the line of her bare shoulder. 'I went into our marriage believing it was forever, but forever has a nasty habit of ending sooner than you think. Then I arrive in Singapore to discover this push-button divorce of yours.' He sounded flippant, but she noticed his tongue sneak out to wet the corner of his mouth. 'It seems that he who hesitates loses his wife without knowing a damn thing about it. That's the way of the computer age. Got a knife handy?'

The touch of his finger, just one tanned finger, had done crazy things to her equilibrium, but Katrin escaped into humour.

'You'd like me to slit your throat after all?'

'Next week. Right now I was thinking more in terms of opening this Pandora's box.' He was nudging the carton with his toe when he frowned. Ruark brought a hand to his eyes and blinked several times, shaking his head.

'What's the matter?' Katrin asked, disturbed by this abrupt distress.

He felt for a chair and sat down, his face drained of colour. 'Nothing. It'll pass.'

She crouched beside him. 'Ruark, tell me the truth. What's happening?' She did not like the way he was opening and closing his eyes as if he was unable to focus.

'All clear,' he said, after a moment. He lay back

his head and gave a strained smile. 'I've been
doing too much close work lately, that's all.'

'Have you seen a doctor?'

'No.'

'You should.'

'Don't be bossy.' He saw her look of concern
and added, 'Maybe I will, once I'm back in
Sydney. Now, please go and get that knife. You
can't keep me in suspense for all eternity.'

Katrin brought him the knife she used for
paring vegetables and watched as he cut carefully
through the binding. When Ruark raised the
cardboard leaves, they stared inside like two
children wondering what Santa had brought.
There was a file, packed with papers, and a
collection of her father's belongings. She
recognised a worn leather writing case, his
tobacco pouch and wallet. Katrin sat the file on
her knee and looked rapidly through. Everything
was arranged in chronological order. There was a
lengthy report detailing her original visit to the
solicitor's office, and carbon copies of letters
Oliver had written, clipped to subsequent replies.
Reading them, she began to silently curse her
stepbrother. She had not known these letters
existed; letters which referred to telephone calls
when Oliver had obviously been pressurising Mr
Beng into speeding the divorce procedure along.
Had her stepbrother guessed her state of mind,
known how fragile her feelings were? Damn him!
How different things might have been if Oliver
had not orchestrated behind the scenes—or
would they?

Katrin frowned, reaching the final sheet in the
file.

'You can't find the decrees,' Ruark deduced.

'So, may I ask, yet again, where the hell are they?'

'I've no idea. Here, you look.' She shoved the file into his lap, furious with herself, furious with Oliver, furious with Ruark. 'Perhaps I've missed them.'

'No, thanks. I'll take your word that they're not in there.'

His evasive action jarred, and she cast him a worried glance. 'Are your eyes still troubling you?'

'Forget my eyes,' he rapped.

'Wouldn't it be wise to consult——?' she began, but the barely controlled fury she saw on his face curtailed any suggestion she had been about to make.

'God, but you're so marvellously inept!' he accused, his whole body tense. He reminded her of a tiger about to spring.

'Can't you understand?' Katrin asked tightly, hating the way he was treating her as if she was a dunce. 'Daddy was on the critical list, and all my energy went into coping with that.'

'In other words, you didn't keep track of our divorce?'

'No! I never realised everything would happen so fast. I imagined there'd be plenty of time, that the legalities would take months and months. I thought I'd be able to—to organise myself once Daddy's crisis was over.' Her voice was growing fainter, but the glare he gave prodded a revolt. 'In any case, the fact I'm unable to conjure up the decrees is a mere technicality. Look!' Katrin grabbed the file back from his knee and leafed through the papers to tap savagely with a finger. 'Here's Mr Beng's account. He lists the dates the decree nisi and decree absolute were issued.'

'If I was Hardy, I'd say this is another fine mess you've gotten us into,' Ruark said, totally unimpressed. He gestured towards the writing case which still lay in the box. 'Try in there.'

'Nothing, just personal stuff,' she said, when she had looked through the assortment of envelopes she found inside. 'Letters from my father's friends. Tomorrow I'll go back to the big house and have another scout round. Oliver may have put the decrees in——' The scornful glitter of his blue eyes made her falter. '—In his desk drawer?'

'Not on your life. He'd never leave something so important lying around. They're probably in a safe box at his bank. That's where I'd keep the damn things. When does he return from Antwerp?'

'Next week supposedly, but he did mention a side trip to London.'

'Great!' His sarcasm was cold.

'If you'd have warned me you were coming to Singapore I would have had time to serve up the decrees on a silver platter,' she shot back.

He ignored her. 'No way am I sitting around waiting for darling Ollie to show. First thing tomorrow morning I shall be beating down Beng's office door. I need legal proof of this divorce, and I want it now! I can't afford any problems later.'

'I suppose not,' Katrin agreed, her depressed spirits now tumbling to low-water mark at this reminder of his eagerness to install a new Mrs Lencioni.

'How long was Felix on the critical list?'

Ruark asked unexpectedly, breaking into the silence.

'Er, six—roughly six weeks,' she stammered, struggling to take the mental leap required.

'Poor devil.'

The concern in Ruark's voice suddenly brought everything back—how frail and pathetic her father had seemed, his twisted face almost transparent against the pillows of the hospital bed. She remembered the agony of wondering if he would die, and later *when* he would die, and her throat stiffened.

'He was drugged,' she said. 'The doctors assured me he wasn't in pain.'

'Perhaps not physically, but emotionally?'

'Emotionally he suffered,' she confirmed, finding it odd that Ruark, who had been so far away at the time, should understand. 'His soul was in his eyes, and all the pain showed through. Oliver told me I was being fanciful, but I wasn't. My father was paralysed so he couldn't talk, but his eyes said everything. I'm sure he knew he was going to die.' Katrin licked her lips. 'At first there was supposed to be a chance of recovery, and it was suggested I chat to him as much as possible. I was meant to keep his spirits up.' She attempted a laugh. 'You never heard such drivel. I was like the Trevi fountain, I never stopped splashing him with words.'

'But he didn't respond?'

'He spoke once,' she admitted. 'Just once.'

'What did he say?'

Her eyes were stupidly wet. Katrin blinked, needing time, but after a gap she spoke. 'Go to Ruark.'

'Dear God!' He plunged his head into his

hands. 'And why didn't you? After he died, I
mean,' he said hoarsely, then his voice strength-
ened and he sat up. 'I'm sorry, that's not fair.'
The subject was dropped. 'You must have given
Felix a great deal of comfort in his last days. He
loved you so damn much.'

'Too much.'

He gave her a strange look and seemed to be on
the brink of questioning her comment, when he
changed his mind. 'Maybe he overcompensated
because you'd never known your mother. Poor
Felix, you wrapped him around your little finger
and——'

'I don't think it was quite like that.'

'Wasn't it?' He shrugged off the idea and
grinned, raising his hand to tug at a wayward curl
lying on her shoulder. 'I wonder what he would
have had to say about this tumbled look of
yours?' His eyes slid to the pert swell of her
breasts. 'And the flashy golden boob tube?'

The deep timbre of his voice held a note
Katrin recognised, and the world seemed to miss
a revolution. There was hunger, sexual hunger,
in his gaze. He leant closer and involved himself
in winding the dark strand of hair around his
finger. If any air was left in her lungs it had
become a high-octane mixture, for the nearness
of Ruark was causing her heart to thump, her
blood to sing.

'He would have approved,' she protested,
unable to move.

'Never. Felix would have said that young
women who dress like this are asking for it.'

'For what?' Katrin dared to ask, though she
knew she shouldn't, knew the question must take
them past the halfway mark.

'This,' he murmured, as his mouth covered hers.

The kiss was long and sweet, filling Katrin with the desperate urge to try and recapture the dream of their lost love. A Spanish girl, now long gone from Singapore, had once said how Ruark was *muy hombre*—very much a man. So he was. And when she was in his arms, she felt so very much a woman. Her hands slid up to his shoulders, one pushing into the thick blue-black hair at the nape of his neck. The familiar hardness of his body was immensely exciting, and she smelled the evocative fragrance of his aftershave, warm and woody, with a rich overtone of spice.

'Oh Ruark,' she sighed, when he pulled back to smile at her.

'Oh, pussycat,' he grinned.

From out of nowhere came the realisation that although this moment was high drama for her, it probably meant little to him. But she didn't care, not when he was stroking his fingertips across the smooth line of her shoulders, bending his head to taste her skin.

'So beautiful,' he murmured, his voice husky. 'You feel like silk, taste like nectar. You always did.'

He kissed her again. This is right, Katrin thought dazedly, her lips parting beneath his. This is what I want, this is where I belong. The wretched months in between faded. She needed to kiss him all over, touch him all over, and——

Ruark's mouth lifted from hers. 'Pussycat,' he whispered against her ear. 'You're such a hard act to follow.'

To follow! She almost sobbed out loud. She

didn't belong in his arms, he had a new bride
waiting in the wings. But she's not on stage yet,
Katrin thought defiantly, and the curtain hasn't
quite come down on me. Almost, but not finally.
His mouth was on her throat, kissing and
nibbling, and his hands began to caress. When
his fingers brushed her breast, a wave of desire
crested. Ruark found the hardening peak and
began touching, then not touching, teasing her
and himself in fond fun. So often in the past they
had taken turns to tease, slowly and inexorably
drawing each other deeper and deeper into a
maelstrom of arousal until passion was paramount. Then they became a fusion of flesh. One
on one. Male and female. Heaven only a hair's
breadth away.

But Katrin didn't want to be teased, not today.
She wanted to be loved, and quickly. She wanted
to lie naked with him, to feel his hands move as
he excited her beyond reason. Scarcely aware of
what she was doing, Katrin curled her fingers
around the edge of the gold lurex and pulled the
boobtube off over her head.

Ruark's eyes were drawn downwards to the
firm, honeyed curves. 'Dear God,' he breathed.
'You shouldn't have done that. I'm vulnerable,
pussycat. Too damned vulnerable.'

For what seemed like forever, his eyes roamed
over her. A muscle clenched in his jaw, then, all
of a sudden, he hauled her back into his arms.
Within seconds Katrin realised all game playing
had ceased. His kiss now was bruising, the hands
which covered her breasts were fevered. Aroused
as she was, she was unprepared for the urgency
she had released. In the past Ruark had valued
his capacity to prolong their lovemaking, always

forestalling his own pleasure until he was sure of hers, but not today.

'Ruark,' she started to protest, but his mouth bit savagely down on hers. Katrin twisted, wanting him to stop, but found herself pinned beneath him on the sofa. 'Wait,' she begged.

'I can't wait,' he groaned, a harsh sound of satisfaction emerging from his throat as his hands moved restlessly over her breasts, his fingers squeezing the rigid peaks until she gasped, half from arousal, half from pain. 'Let me,' he insisted, and ripped away the barriers of clothing which were between them.

The rasp of his breathing filled her ears, the weight of his body crushed hers. His mastery was relentless and, despite herself, Katrin knew her body was starting to respond, set aflame by the sheer carnality of his actions. Gripping her hips with both hands to hold her captive, Ruark took what he wanted. In an uncontrollable spasm he jerked against her, and then sagged. Katrin felt chilled. A bleakness entered her heart. She lay there, slowly dying.

'Forgive me?' Ruark pleaded, his lips moving on her brow.

She kept her eyes closed. 'It doesn't matter.'

He sighed. 'Of course it matters. I've really loused things up, haven't I? I haven't done that since—since I was a teenager. I pride myself on being a reliable practitioner of the art, but I must be cracking up. Hell, first my eyes start playing tricks and now I can't even make love decently.'

Katrin gritted her teeth. 'I said it doesn't matter.'

'It matters to me.'

'Fine, it matters to you but I couldn't give a

damn,' she declared and extricated herself from
beneath him.

She felt hurt and confused, yet had to admit
that what had just happened could be reasonably
said to be as much her fault as his. Katrin dressed
at speed, determined she would shovel Ruark
from her apartment post haste, and never mind
good manners. She was waiting impatiently while
he took his turn in the bathroom, when the
telephone rang.

'Good afternoon.' She had answered blandly,
but straight away felt like braying with frustration
when her caller turned out to be Mrs Ho. 'No, I
don't mind you ringing me at home. Yes, the new
photographs of Lisu are excellent.' She was lying
on both counts. Over the past two days Ruark's
presence, and her search for the documents, had
meant nothing much else had mattered. She had
yet to get around to looking through the new
portfolio. 'I'll speak to Lisu about them in the
morning, when she comes for her hair and make-
up class,' Katrin promised, trying not to sound
too tart, but Mrs Ho was immune to her mood,
and talked on and on.

She managed to end the conversation just as
Ruark joined her in the living room. To her
dismay she saw that although his jeans had been
pulled on, he was bare-chested. Her heart
stopped beating. How well she remembered the
gleam of his skin, the crispness of the covering of
dark hair.

He held out a hand and smiled. 'I promise I'm
in control of my reflexes now. Let's go to bed,
Kat, and I'll make love to you in the way you
deserve to be made love to. It'll be good, like the
old times.'

She kept her distance. 'No.'

'Look, I apologise.' The pink tip of his tongue sought the edge of his mouth. 'Believe me, I'd move mountains to change what's just happened. But you set me on fire and it's been such a long time since——'

'Forget it.' She rejected his excuses. 'We should never have been making love in the first place. We *are* divorced.'

'Are we?' He took a step forwards and planted himself only a yard away, feet set apart. 'I have yet to see any proof, and in any case I don't feel divorced.'

'That's because you've not had time yet to become used to the idea. But I have,' she added defensively.

Ruark raised a dark brow. 'And yet you bared your breasts for me?'

All she could do was pretend he had never spoken. 'As far as I'm concerned, we've been divorced for approaching a year.'

Ruark rubbed his hand up and down his arm, drawing her attention to the dragon emblazoned there. 'You can't deny something still exists between us.'

Katrin refused to respond. 'You came back to Singapore in order to secure a divorce, and we are divorced. Once the decrees have been found, you'll be on your way.'

'Back Down Under,' he agreed, with such ease that Katrin felt extremely irritated. 'Can you tell me where this Mr Beng hangs out?'

'Chinatown,' she said, as he reached for his shirt.

'Where in Chinatown?'

Katrin picked up the correspondence file and

thumbed through. 'I can't remember the name of
the street, but it'll be in here. Damn,' she said,
after a moment or two. 'Only a post office box
number is given on his letter heading. Hold on a
sec, his address'll be in the phone book.'

'Well?' Ruark asked, when she had worked her
way down three long pages of Bengs.

'Sorry, but I can't seem to trace him,' she
admitted, feeling prickly because any matter
which involved her and Ruark seemed destined to
go wrong. 'I know he calls himself Benny Beng,
but that's not his given name. I don't know his
correct Chinese name, or even an initial. He
could be any one of the hundreds of Bengs listed
here.'

'Ring-a-ding-ding,' he drawled facetiously.
'First an elusive divorce, and now an elusive
solicitor. What do you bet tomorrow morning I'll
be stuck with a taxi driver who doesn't have a
single word of English, and spend hours on some
dead-end search?'

'I know where his offices are, I could take you
there,' Katrin offered, feeling it was her duty.
'But the morning's out. I have a class from ten
until eleven, and afterwards I'm compèring the
show at the Regent. Suppose we meet up at the
hotel   around   two-thirty   and   head   for
Chinatown?'

Ruark finished buttoning up his shirt and
shrugged. 'Do I have any choice?' he asked.

CHAPTER FOUR

KATRIN flicked down the intercom key. 'Michelle, please could you bring in Lisu's new photographs, and ask her to come and see me before she goes home?'

The morning class had finished, now she was cramming as much as she could into the time available prior to her departure for the Regent. She heard a slight hesitation before her receptionist answered.

'But the photographs have already been despatched.'

'Despatched? Where to?'

'The DeSouza competition. Mr Oliver filled out the entry form and I mailed it,' the girl explained eagerly, 'together with Lisu's new portfolio.'

'The interfering so-and-so.' Katrin's mumble heralded murder. 'When was this?'

'Lunchtime, earlier in the week. Mr Oliver came in while you were at the Regent.'

'Why was I not informed?'

Michelle's enthusiasm faltered. 'He said the entry was to be a surprise.'

'It is!'

A tinny giggle filled the silence. When in doubt, Michelle giggled. 'Lisu's here now,' she said, with a gush of relief. 'Shall I send her in?'

'Please. And just remember in future it's important I know everything which happens in the name of the agency. I've told you before to ignore Mr Oliver's instructions. *I'm* the boss.'

'Yes, Mrs Lencioni. I'm sorry, Mrs Lencioni.'
Her receptionist was properly subdued.

A knock came at the door, and Lisu entered.
For an uncertain moment she hovered then, at
Katrin's bidding, walked forward to perch herself
on the edge of a chair.

'I understand your photographs have been
submitted for the DeSouza competition,' Katrin
said. 'Was this with your knowledge?'

'Mr Oliver consulted my mother. She was
delighted to give permission.'

Mrs Ho again! Katrin smothered a groan. 'Did
you want your name to be entered?'

'I won't win.'

'But what happens if you do?'

'I won't,' the girl said doggedly, and her pale
fingers began to twist.

Katrin gave up, changing the subject to Lisu's
progress in her various classes. Maybe she was
worrying about something which would never
happen. Maybe the gods would be sympathetic
and downgrade Mrs Ho's beautiful daughter to
an also-ran.

After the girl had gone, Katrin made a rapid
review of the circumstances which had led up to
Lisu's entry in the competition. In future, she
decided, she must deny her stepbrother access to
the agency. She could see no alternative. She had
never felt comfortable about the way Oliver
marched around the Pivotelle suite, acting like a
feudal lord about to exercise his *droit de
seigneur*, and this latest high-handedness was too
much. But informing him he was to keep away
would not be easy. He would be mortally
offended. There was a sickening moment of
apprehension, when she thought how poisonous

he could be. Unlike Ruark, his displeasure wasn't brought out into the open—whoosh!—and then over. Instead Oliver's anger festered long after the original upset, cropping up in sharp acts of vengeance. He was not a man to cross.

Katrin accepted that in the past she had tended to opt for the easy way out. Head-on clashes had been avoided. Yes, there had been skirmishes, but she had never gone point blank against him. Why? Partly because Oliver had been so tied into her life that friction, any friction, was unwelcome, and partly because he was older and a far more forceful personality than she. She turned a pencil between her fingers, wondering if perhaps her attitude didn't boil down to one thing—cowardice? At heart was she spineless, like her father? He had never fought a single battle in his life.

Muriel, Oliver's short, plump and blue-rinsed mother, had swooped on the unsuspecting Felix and installed him in her eyrie before he had realised what was happening. He had been a widower for seventeen years, and would have contentedly remained so if Muriel hadn't been placed beside him at a dinner party. Five years of widowhood, with no-one to boss, was as much as she could stand, and once she had assured herself that Felix was honest, had clean fingernails, and changed his underwear without being told, she took charge. Whether or not he had wanted to be married for a second time was immaterial. It was suggested he buy her an engagement ring—so he did. It was suggested he buy her a wedding ring— so he did. Invitations were despatched, the ceremony took place, and Felix and Katrin moved into the big house to make up a foursome with Muriel and Oliver. Muriel had the take-

charge manner reminiscent of sergeant-majors,
but Felix enjoyed being taken charge of. When
she had died, two short years later, he had been a
broken reed. He had needed help.

'Do you think it would be a good idea if we
moved to England?' he had asked Katrin at dinner
one night, shortly after the funeral. 'How about a
little cottage, maybe in the West Country?'

Oliver had wafted Ah Lan and her dish of
snow-peas away. 'And you'd grow roses together?'
he had intervened.

The older man had not noticed the sneer.

'If you agree, Katrin, a move might be
beneficial,' Felix had suggested, giving her a look
which begged agreement. 'Life in the East tends
to be artificial as far as Westerners are concerned.
You've never known what it is to look after
yourself, because there's always been an amah
lurking in the background.' He had reached
across to pat her hand. 'Could be, my love, it's
time you came down to earth and got to grips
with real values. If we lived in England you'd
learn to fend for yourself.'

'You mean she'd learn to plough fields, muck
out cows, spread fertiliser round those damn
roses?' Oliver had enquired.

This time Felix had detected the derision and,
flush-faced, he had bent back to his plate.

'Don't be sarcastic,' Katrin had said, coming to
the rescue. 'Daddy's point is valid. If he wants to
leave Singapore and settle in England, that suits
me fine.'

Oliver had downed his knife and fork. 'And
what happens to that model agency we launched
not so long ago?' He had said 'we' but both
Katrin and her father knew he meant *I*.

'Pivotelle could be sold,' she had suggested.

His fingers had snapped. 'Just like that?'

'It might take time, but——'

'Oliver's right,' Felix had cut in. 'We can't just abandon everything, our future is here. Besides, an old dog doesn't change its tricks. I'd probably be miserable back in England.'

'I don't see why,' Katrin had protested, in an attempt to counteract her stepbrother's quick nod of agreement.

'Yes, I would,' Felix confirmed, saying what he knew Oliver was mentally prompting him to say. 'Instead, suppose the two of us find a nice apartment here, on the coast.'

Oliver had laughed. 'Have you the faintest idea how much a seaside apartment costs in Singapore?'

'Well, I haven't made enquiries, but——'

'You'd need to be a millionaire to afford something half decent,' Oliver had replied, granting Felix a condescending smile. 'Forget such foolishness. Muriel would have insisted you and Katrin remain under my roof, and you'd both be doing me a great favour if you'd agree to that course of action. I have plenty of room. And if you went, my dear old chap, who would I have to beat at backgammon?'

Katrin's father had laughed heartily, and leaving the big house, or Singapore, had never been mentioned again.

Traffic build-up had slowed them to a crawl, and when a cloying aroma of incense filled the car Katrin glanced out. They were beside an Indian temple, a spectacular tower of entwined, garishly painted figures rising above the entrance. She frowned. The temple and its tower were familiar, but not much else. Chinatown, a crumbling maze of narrow streets and alleyways which huddled against the banks of the Singapore River, was diminishing rapidly. Turn-of-the-century shophouses, ancient go-downs, Taoist shrines and other reminders of old China, were being bulldozed down daily, to be supplanted with uniform multi-storey concrete blocks.

'I thought you knew where to find Beng's offices?' Ruark commented from the passenger seat.

'I thought so, too.' She did a silent but desperate calculation and turned left, bringing them into a crevice between two brand-new towers of government flats. Katrin squinted up, searching for a street name on the side of the building, but no luck. All she could see were forests of horizontal bamboo poles jutting below windows, each decked with colourful washing. 'Perhaps if we head west?'

He shrugged. 'Don't ask me. I'm afraid I'm adrift. Everything's changed since the last time I was here.'

'Likewise,' she muttered glumly.

'Do you remember that market we went to once, where an old woman was eager to sell me a brace of bats?' Ruark chuckled at the memory. 'She guaranteed they'd make a nourishing broth. Better than Heinz, she said.'

Katrin laughed. 'Yes, I do. But the food markets in the streets have disappeared now, and the night markets, the *pasar malam*. These days you shop in sanitised escalatored precincts, with little colour or clangour, and it's not half the fun.'

After a right turn, and a left, she sighed.

'Lost?' he enquired.

'More or less.'

Ruark shifted in his seat to speak to her. 'I hate to cast a blight, but the law of averages tells me Mr Beng's offices have been razed to the ground.'

She felt a bubble of panic. 'If so, he'll have moved somewhere else.' She eased off the accelerator. 'Driving around like this is hopeless. I'll find a parking space, and then we can go and make enquiries. I know most of the buildings are new, but I'd swear his offices were in this locality.'

'Were isn't the same as are,' Ruark pointed out. He sounded so offhand that he provoked a short-tempered reaction.

'Don't blame me for this urban redevelopment, or whatever it's called,' Katrin snapped, and stamped on the brake. A car ahead had pulled out from the kerb, so she swung the Ford into the vacant slot and cut the engine. 'I didn't choose to change the face of the Island overnight.'

'Neither did you choose to come to Hong Kong with me when I asked,' he murmured.

'Asked!' Her voice cracked. 'You never asked. You——'

'There's a policeman.' Ruark pointed through the window to where an impressively turbanned Sikh sat astride a motorcycle. 'Let's see if he's heard of this elusive Mr Beng.'

'Oh yes, sir,' the policeman said, when he had listened to Ruark's enquiry. 'I am acquainted with the gentleman. He had splendid offices just along from the old noodle factory.'

'That's the right Mr Beng,' Katrin agreed, beaming with relief at having pinned the solicitor down at last. She was almost tempted to stick her tongue out at Ruark and go, '*There*, he does exist.'

'Wonderful offices,' the policeman mused. 'I remember there were two white marble lions guarding the entrance. Splendid creatures, about eight feet tall.'

'I understand he'd had them shipped from China,' Katrin added enthusiastically.

'Gone now,' the policeman told her. 'Both the lions and Benny Beng have gone. All disappeared. My word, what a crook that man was, an absolute bounder. If we ever catch up with him, oh dear, oh dear.' He wobbled his head to indicate dire punishment.

Ruark's blue eyes met Katrin's startled violet ones for a moment, before he turned back to the policeman. 'You mean Beng has done a bunk?'

'Last heard of in deepest Borneo. He'll never be found in a month of veritable Sundays.'

Katrin opened her mouth, then closed it again. Doubts about the mechanics of the divorce had pricked spasmodically ever since Ruark had first asked to see the decrees, but she had managed to ignore them. The policeman's revelation changed all that. The pricks were now stabs, and Katrin felt queasy.

'What did Mr Beng do?' she forced herself to ask.

'What didn't he do? He filed false claims on behalf of false clients. He avoided paying tax. He demanded money for work he'd never done.' The Sikh chuckled, warming to his subject. 'He charged exorbitant fees. He swindled his customers right, left and centre. In fact, he broke every rule in the book.'

'So who's been brought in to take charge?' asked Ruark. 'We require some information about a matter he handled. Who can help us?'

'I regret to report, sir, no-one.'

'No-one?' Katrin bleated, the world crashing about her ears.

'No, ma'am.'

'But someone must have access to his files,' Ruark insisted.

'There are no files, sir. We don't know whether the scoundrel burned them, or if they're buried beneath a new housing complex. When his offices were demolished, the paperwork vanished without trace. Benny Beng had advertised in the press that he would be switching to new premises, but he never put in an appearance there. Neither did his files.'

'So what do we do?' Katrin wailed, with Brechtian pathos.

Ruark put his arm around her shoulders and gave an encouraging squeeze. 'Cheer up. All is not lost. The courts must have a record.' He smiled at the policeman. 'Thanks for your help. My wife and I are most grateful.'

'I'm not your wife,' she said bleakly, as they climbed back into the car.

'A slip of the tongue.' He threw her a sideways look. 'But you might be, you know.'

'I might not!'

'You heard what the man said.'

'He didn't say Mr Beng defrauded *all* his clients,' she protested, grabbing for a lifebelt. 'You've seen the letters I received. You've seen his report.'

'Agreed, but there's still a gaping hole— anything official.'

Katrin hooked her fingers around the steering wheel and held on tight. There was too much to absorb right now, she was only skimming the implications.

'This is all your fault,' she announced, aware she was being illogical and unjust, but needing to hit back against something, someone. 'If only you'd done everything properly. If you'd been here and gone to the solicitor with me. If you'd stayed around to——'

'If we'd stayed together, do you think we would have ever needed a solicitor?' he asked. 'Or would we have worked out a solution to our problems? I think we would.'

'That's totally irrelevant,' she stormed. 'You're the one who shot off to Hong Kong, pursuing your career with such damnable single-mindedness.'

'And you're the wife who chose not to join her husband,' he remarked.

'You gave me one chance. Only one!'

'Did I?' he drawled.

'Yes! You forced events to crisis level, and because I didn't click my heels immediately and rush to do your bidding, you left.'

'Are you aware that the Chinese character for crisis has two components—danger and possibility?' Ruark questioned.

His calm made her want to yell with impotent rage. How could he sound so matter-of-fact, when she needed to draw blood?

'No, I'm not. And what's more, I don't care.'

'But it's important. Creating a crisis was risky, I admit, but I think subconsciously I was attempting to open up new avenues. I wanted to release us from the trap we were in.' He rubbed his fingers across his jaw. 'Some people eat chips with everything, and in the latter months of our time together we seemed to have rows with everything. But there were too many negative vibes at the big house for us to have a chance.'

'Did you make all that up yourself, or are you paraphrasing a pet psychiatrist?' she demanded tartly.

'It's good old homespun philosophy, pussycat,' he said with a grin. 'Fifteen months on your own leaves a lot of spare time for thinking.'

'But you weren't on your own. What about the girl who throws rocks at wallabies?' Katrin wished she had a rock handy herself.

'Okay, nine months alone,' he adjusted. 'What say we head for the divorce courts?'

She took in a deep breath and found a soupçon of calm. 'I can't, not right now. I'm afraid I don't have time. Arlene volunteered to oversee things at the agency because Michelle's not too happy at being left on her own, but——' She inspected her wristwatch. 'I really must get back there before five. A business doesn't run itself, and I did take time off yesterday afternoon as well.' She managed an apologetic smile. 'I'm sorry.'

'That's okay. I realise you have commitments.' He saw her looking at him beneath her lashes. 'Male chauvinist I may be in your opinion, but I don't always see things entirely from my own point of view.' He threw her a fast grin, the kind of grin that in their courtship days would have kept her happy for twenty-four hours. 'At a guess, I'd say right now you feel as if your intestines are being drawn out on a windlass, like St Elmo's. And like mine!'

He had always been able to make her laugh at the most unlikely moments, and Katrin giggled.

'Dead right. Look, suppose I make a quick detour and drop you off near the courts? You can ring me at Pivotelle, or at home, when you know the worst.'

Ruark fixed her with a long, intent look. 'But what is the worst, Kat? Being divorced, or finding that you're still married to me?'

The sixty-four thousand dollar question, she thought, and could not produce an answer. Ten minutes' later, Katrin deposited him at the appropriate junction and headed for the agency.

'Are you okay?' Arlene asked, when she walked in the door.

'I'm fine.' She saw her friend's concern and wondered if she should explain the whole sorry mess. But how could she? Where would she begin? And why start a tale when the final sentence was as yet unknown? She pushed strands of dark hair out of her eyes. 'Anything important crop up while I've been out?'

'Nothing I couldn't handle.' Arlene handed her a piece of paper. 'These are details of the phone calls, together with the action I took.' She frowned at Katrin's strained expression and overbright eyes. 'Slap me on the wrist if I'm interfering, but should Ruark have this effect on you? Ever since he arrived you've been leaping around as though your tail was plugged into an electric socket.'

'You don't understand. There are ... complications,' she said evasively.

'I understand one thing.'

Katrin started to read the list. 'And what's that?'

'You're still in love with him.'

'Can't I keep anything secret from you?' she joked, but tears were suddenly near. She kept her head down and blinked hard.

''Fraid not, Kat.' The older woman's voice was gentle. 'Watching what you're going through is like watching myself when Bob and I split. That first year alone was pretty flaky, and I still hate being divorced. Whenever I hear a mention of how happy he is with his second wife, I want to commit hari-kari. Why on earth I didn't swallow my pride and beg him to let us try again, I'll never know.' Arlene sighed. 'Take my advice. If you're longing for him, for heaven's sake stretch out a hand. Don't be proud. Pride can be destructive, and that's straight from the horse's mouth. If you want another chance, you'll have to tell him how you feel.'

'I can't.'

'Why not? I know it's a risk, and you may end up with egg on your face, but——'

'Ruark's getting married again!' she blurted out.

'Oh, my God! When?'

'I don't know.' Katrin suddenly realised that if the divorce had not gone through, it would take many months before Ruark would be free and able to marry the rock-throwing girl. 'Not for a while, maybe.'

Arlene brightened, and said snappily, 'Then hone your weapons.'

'I beg your pardon?'

'Use your feminine wiles. He fell in love with you once, make him fall in love with you again. Ruark is a priceless pearl of a man. Letting him go the first time was careless, to do it a second time would be criminal.' The blonde's grin was wide. 'And if you don't intend to lay claim, move over and give someone else a chance. Older women and young men are the "in" thing. He and I would make a fantastic couple. Though, in actual fact, Ruark's not that much younger than me. I thought

I noticed the first trace of furrows on his handsome brow, so maybe he's beginning to run to seed?'

'He is not!'

Arlene laughed at such a heated defence. 'Then go get him, girl.'

She drove back through the rush-hour traffic like a zombie. She had stayed on at Pivotelle until five-thirty, willing him to call, but the phone had remained silent. What could she gather from this lack of contact? Was she a divorcée? Was she still Ruark's wife? The scenario went awry. Katrin's habit of driving on the assumption she was the only sane person on the road stood her in good stead, and, despite operating with three-parts of her mind elsewhere, she managed to orienteer herself and the Ford back to the apartment in one piece.

'Hello, pussycat,' Ruark said in his familiar malt-whisky voice, materialising beside her as she climbed out of the car.

Her heart thudded out of tempo. 'Did you see the records?' she cried.

'The short answer is—yes.'

'And?'

'And I think we should go up to your apartment.' He steered her aside as two joggers in tracksuits and sweatbands dashed by. 'I wouldn't want you to break down in public. You look as if you're about to buckle at the knees.'

The minutes in the lift, pressed among half-a-dozen fellow tenants, were the most tormented in Katrin's entire life. She kept sneaking glances at Ruark, hoping to find clues in his expression, but had no success. Was he disappointed? Was he relieved? Sensing her stress, he winked, and she wondered frantically what message he was conveying. By the time they reached her door, she didn't much care which way the dice fell. All that mattered was an end to not knowing.

'Well?' she gasped.

Ruark put his arm around her shoulders, leading her along the hall and into the living room. 'Sit down before you fall down,' he commanded, and dumped her into an armchair.

'Well?' she demanded again, as he sat opposite.

'I saw the records. In fact, I went through every case the divorce courts have dealt with over the past two years, three times over.' His tongue caught briefly in the corner of his mouth. 'There was no trace of Lencioni versus Lencioni.'

'Oh!'

'After I'd done that, I requested an audience with the highest-ranking official who was available. A judge was on the premises, but I had to wait an hour until he was free to see me. I explained the situation and he told me categorically that if a couple aren't listed, then they haven't been granted a divorce. Each decree is numbered in sequence, and together we checked to make sure every number had been used. They had. There were no Lencionis.'

'Oh!'

'The judge also reckoned your villain, Benny Beng, never handled divorce cases. Marine matters, land purchase and building work were far more lucrative for him.'

'Oh!'

Ruark had held his feelings in check long enough. Now they fractured. 'Is that all you have to say?' he demanded, his voice harsh.

Katrin nodded. 'My brain cells appear to have disintegrated.'

'You're damn right they have! I'd say they disintegrated the day you set about concocting this phony divorce. You paid a single visit to Beng, and you imagined that was all it took? Didn't it cross your mind that your presence might be required in court?'

Colour flamed her cheeks. 'You can get mail order divorces these days,' she protested, in an effort to vindicate herself. 'Besides, I've already told you how everything got out of hand.'

'You were dismantling our marriage, and you paid not one jot of attention? The way you've treated the manner is unbelievable,' he berated. 'You've been so damned . . . nonchalant!'

Katrin fought back. 'That might be your choice of word, but it's not mine. I've explained what happened, and why.'

She knew her explanation did not ring quite true, but there was nothing she could do about that. There were limits to what she was prepared to reveal.

'Some explanation!' Ruark leapt from his chair like a wild beast, and scooped down to catch hold of her jaw, forcing her to look up into the angriest blue eyes she had ever seen. 'You've managed to screw up my life well and truly.'

'Ditto!'

Her prompt rebellion seemed unexpected. He frowned and, after a moment, released her. With a deep sigh, he turned and paced to the glass doors which opened on to the balcony, where he examined the sky.

'I suppose there are what could be termed "plus points",' he said after a minute or two.

Katrin eyed his broad back warily. 'Like what?'

He turned to face her. 'Like visualising how

hopping mad Ollie's going to be when he discovers what's happened, or rather what *hasn't* happened. And——' He paused, a thread of masculine intent in his voice. Katrin was suspended in a tense time-warp as she waited for what came next. 'And like me being given clearance to claim my marital rights once again.'

She froze, fear and excitement simultaneously flowing through her. His statement, so confidently given, made her as panicky as hell.

'Don't threaten me,' she protested.

Ruark laughed. 'I can hardly be accused of threatening my own wife by saying I want to go to bed with her.' He lifted an eyebrow. 'You never complained in the past. As I remember, you initiated the proceedings yourself, on more than one occasion.'

'That was then.' Her pulses raced as he squatted down beside her, for there was no mistaking that roguish gleam in his eyes. 'But everything's different now. Don't forget about that girl you're going to marry,' Katrin added hastily, when he pushed back the hem of her white linen skirt to expose two bare tanned knees.

'Grr.' He lunged forward. Half a kiss, half a bite, whatever he did to her, the feel of his open mouth on her leg made Katrin's breath come quicker.

'Ruark, don't,' she protested. She knew there must be a hundred good reasons why they should not make love, but could not summon a single one to mind. All she could do was repeat, 'What about that girl you're going to marry?'

'What about her? She's in the future, but you're here, now.' His long hard fingers slid beneath her skirt to touch her inner thigh. 'Mmm, silk. Warm silk. I always did have a fetish about your legs, and other parts of you.' He inserted a fingertip under the edge of her white lace briefs. 'Many other parts.'

'This isn't right,' she said, pushing his hand away, but a tell-tale tremble marred the cool tone she had striven for.

'On the contrary, it's exactly right.' He kissed first one knee, and then the other. 'Don't worry, I have no intention of rushing things. This time, pussycat, I intend to wait until you're so aroused that you're pleading with me to——'

'It's morally wrong!' Katrin cried, despising the fire which was beginning to run in her veins. 'You can't make love to me when there's some other woman lined up.'

'Can't I? Just watch. Short of nuclear attack, nothing's going to stop us from going into your bedroom and on to your bed, and doing again what we used to do so marvellously well before. How long ago did you last make love?' Ruark enquired. 'And don't count that fiasco yesterday.'

'I—I haven't,' she muttered uncomfortably. She knew she must get up and walk out of the room, that staying still was suicidal. But she just sat there.

'Not since me?' His eyes were suddenly tender. He lifted her hand and kissed the palm. 'Oh Kat, darling! Thank you for that.' His smile came back, even more assured. 'Well, I don't pretend we can make up for fifteen months in one fell swoop, but if at first we don't succeed, we can try, try, try again.'

His hand moved to her breast, a fingertip caressing the pointed outline beneath the flimsy white silk. Katrin closed her eyes. She wasn't breathing air any longer, she was breathing sensuality. A hot wild sweetness was flooding her body, seeping down from her breast to her thighs. All she could think of was how much she had missed the taste of Ruark, the feel of Ruark, the thrust of Ruark. She needed that again. She needed to fondle him, to run her hands across his warm skin, to clutch at his hip as she dragged him closer, deeper. Once more she wanted to kiss the silvered scars at brow and shoulder and pelvis.

'Strip for me, pussycat,' Ruark murmured, and her eyes shot open. Her surprise seemed to amuse him because he grinned. 'It's hardly an original request. You never used to be shy.' He took hold of her hand and brought it to the neck of her blouse. 'A kiss for every button freed, and here's one to start.'

He leaned forward and kissed her, a kiss which made her head spin, a kiss which brought his lips to the very edge of her soul. What secret aphrodisiac do his pores exude, Katrin wondered, as she found herself haltingly start to obey his command. A button was opened. A kiss was given. Again and again, in sensual repetition. By the time Katrin slid the silk from her shoulders, she was breathless.

'The next time we're together, dispense with underwear,' Ruark said throatily, watching as she reached around her back to unfasten her white lace bra. 'I like to think of you naked beneath your clothes. Naked for me.'

'There won't be a next time,' she found the strength to say, but he just raised his brows and looked at her. 'There won't!'

'Pussycat,' he demurred, and pulled her up out of the chair and into his arms. He kissed her mouth and then her throat, softly, yet firmly enough for her to know that tomorrow she would bear the marks of his passion. Then his blue-black head went down, his mouth seeking out the sensitive points of her breast. With a tormented groan Katrin plunged her fingers into the thickness of his hair, holding him close as his tongue curled across her skin. She gasped out loud, her body moving into an involuntary shudder.

'Bed, my darling.' Ruark lifted her into his arms, and by the time they reached the lavendar-and-white bedroom many more kisses had been exchanged. She did not want to leave his embrace, but he set her down. 'Carry on undressing,' he said in a husky voice. Katrin complied, and he gazed sombrely as she stepped out of her skirt and briefs. 'Such a beautiful lady,' he murmured, when she was nude.

He pulled her down beside him on to the bed and began stroking his hands over her, as though he was convincing himself that this was the same woman he had made love to on so many glorious occasions in the past. He pressed his face into her hair, absorbing the fragrance of the glossy curls, then began to kiss her face, her shoulders, her breasts. Ruark moved languorously down her body, savouring each delight, until Katrin moaned in impatience.

'Kiss me *there*,' she whispered, guiding him to the most erotic parts of her. She writhed beneath the bliss of his lips. 'Darling, that feels so good.'

'Pussycat,' he sighed, as he probed her soft sweetness.

The caress of Ruark's mouth, the touch of his hands, made her forget everything. Her passion

mounted and when—was it seconds, or minutes,
or hours later?—he raised his head, she groaned.

'Don't stop. Please don't stop.'

'Katrin, I need to get undressed,' he reminded
her with a fond smile, and she lay in agonised
suspense as he removed his clothes.

Fifteen months had not changed him. Ruark
was still deeply tanned, still wide of shoulder, flat
of belly, lean of hip. She welcomed him back, her
arms wide, and her hands slid over him in an
orgy of delight. These were the muscles she
remembered so well. This was the solid chest
with its rough smattering of black hair. She
purred, then moved restlessly, wanting him to
take her. Somehow their roles had reversed.
Yesterday Ruark had been the animal on heat
who had needed satisfaction rapidly, but now
Katrin was desperate for fulfilment.

'Ruark,' she moaned, when he drew back and
pushed himself up on to one elbow to smile
down at her. This was the Ruark of old, his
own need tightly leashed. 'I want you now,' she
pouted.

He only laughed, tracing a fingertip around the
swollen dark-red tip of her breast at a measured
pace. 'Be patient,' he ordered softly.

'I can't.' She felt as if she had been swept up in
a whirlwind of desire, and was being tossed this
way and that.

'You can. Open your eyes and look at me.'

Lids squeezed tight, she rolled her head back
and forth on the pillow. If he didn't love her, and
quickly, she would splinter into a thousand
pieces. 'No. I need you now, darling.'

'And you'll have me—soon.'

'*Now.*' In a frenzy of need, she raised herself

from the pillow and nipped her teeth into the bulge of his shoulder muscle.

'You bitch!' he exclaimed, but he was laughing as he tumbled her down beneath him, subduing her with fierce, sweet kisses until she lay obedient and gasping beneath him. 'That's my pussycat,' he said, stroking her hair. 'You're making the same mistake I made yesterday, thinking only of yourself.'

He began kissing her again, but calming kisses which rid her of the frenetic energy which had had her shaking and clawing. Minutes past, and his mouth and hands, moving expertly in control, transformed the quicksilver into deep flowing gold.

'I've missed you so much,' Katrin said raggedly, as he ran a long finger down the indent of her spine.

'And I, you.'

Katrin kissed his brow, the scar which ripped across his shoulder, and moved to press her lips against his thigh. When Ruark could stand the pleasure no more he groaned, drawing her up beside him. His body thrust into hers and he took possession. Sensation was all—hot, moist, dizzying sensation. They clung together, crying out in ecstasy as their bodies clenched into magnificent union.

Regret arrived quickly. The moment he left her and made for the bathroom, Katrin felt bereft. She pushed her head into the pillow and acknowledged that she was a fool.

'What did I do that for?' she muttered angrily.

Ruark had suggested a tumble in the hay and she had obliged him not once, but twice! She wondered if the only reason he had wanted to make love to her today was to prove to himself that he was still an expert in bed. He was, but so what? Where did that leave her? Convinced more than ever that Ruark was, and always would be, the only man for her, Katrin wanted to bawl like a baby. Why hadn't she gone with him to Hong Kong fifteen months ago? Because she had had her priorities all wrong, that was why!

She found a tissue and blew her nose. Again she told herself that she would survive without him. No! she would do far more than merely survive. She would sell the agency, cut her ties with Singapore, and travel the big wide world. Her father had been right—she had spent most of her life on a rarefied cloud. Broadening her horizons now seemed a necessity. She would buy a rucksack and march off across the causeway into Malaysia, and then on into Thailand. Plenty of girls tramped Asia on their own. Or should she try her luck as a model in New York or London? And how about acquiring a second husband? Her spirits sank. She didn't want a second husband. She wanted Ruark.

'Cursing me or yourself?' he asked, coming back into the bedroom.

She had heard the noise of the shower, and now that he was dressed again he looked disgustingly refreshed. Katrin twisted the sheet under her armpits and sat up.

'Neither,' she retorted, seeing in his grin the smug satisfaction of a man who had achieved his objective. 'We had what you call "a tumble in the hay", that's all. Don't make it into a big thing.'

He shot her a glance. 'I'm not, pussycat. But are you?' Katrin found the comment unworthy of an answer, or so she told herself. He bent to pop a quick kiss on her mouth, and grinned when she flinched. 'Like the cad I am, I'm afraid I must love you and leave you. I have a dinner date. Like to guess who with?' he teased, when she remained silent.

'No,' Katrin said through clenched teeth, and swore she would murder him if he now revealed that the rock-throwing girl had come to town.

'Then I'll tell you.' He was laughing at her, the blue eyes sparkling as he picked up her comb and ran it through his hair. 'With my Number Two favourite lady—Arlene.'

FREE

4 BOOKS AND A SURPRISE GIFT

Here's a sweetheart of an offer that will put a smile on your lips... and 4 free Harlequin romances in your hands. Plus you'll get a secret gift, as well.

As a subscriber, you'll receive 6 new books to preview every month. Always before they're available in stores. Always for less than the retail price. Always with the right to return the shipment and owe nothing.

YES

Please send me 4 **free** Harlequin Presents novels and my **free** surprise gift. Then send me 6 new Harlequin Presents each month. Bill me for only $1.75 each (for a total of $10.50 per shipment — a savings of $1.20 off the retail price) with no extra charges for shipping and handling. I can return a shipment and cancel anytime. The 4 free books and surprise gift are mine to keep!

106 ClP BA5U

NAME_____

ADDRESS_____APT._____

CITY_____

STATE_____ZIP CODE_____

CHAPTER FIVE

SHE could raise no response to his lighthearted
farewell. As the door closed behind him, the
apartment metamorphised into a wasteland.
Katrin took a ragged breath. So she was still
Ruark's wife. How ironical! How excruciatingly
hysterical! She wanted to shriek and sob and
scream with deranged laughter. Time after time
hadn't she vowed she would sell her soul, to the
devil if need be, if such a status could be achieved
again? And yet now her insides were being
scraped raw. She might be here and now as far
as satisfying his lust was concerned, but she
had scant significance in his long-term affections.
His wife she was—but on a deadly interim
basis.

The motions of showering and dressing were
attended to, and as time passed she began to try
and pull herself together. She was in the middle
of scrambling eggs for supper when it struck her
that her feelings in the wake of their passion
could have been distorted. Katrin undertook a
haphazard rearrangement of her thoughts. Maybe
Ruark's motivation in making love had not been
selfishness? Could he have given such deep
satisfaction if he did not care something for her?
She remembered how he had called her his
darling, and hadn't he vowed he had missed her?
In the past Ruark had always told the truth.
Honest, often to a point of ruthlessness, he had
never conformed to the 'white lie' triteness of

society. He refused to trot out meaningless phrases in order to flatter or ease his path. Whenever he gave an opinion, or offered a comment, for good or bad, he was sincere.

Knowing that, how could Ruark reconcile making love to her if he was committed to another woman? Something was at odds. He could never have pounced on her with such manic intensity the first time, nor held her so tenderly in his arms the second, if his future lay elsewhere. Or could he? The more Katrin scrutinised his words and actions over the past few days, the less likely it seemed. A tiny flame of hope began to flicker.

Ruark had never bothered to disguise the fact that his attraction towards her remained a vibrant pull. But what bearing did this have on his relationship with the Australian girl, a girl he had spoken about in the most offhand terms? She did not know. Katrin continued her review. 'How could you do this to me?' he had raged on hearing of the divorce. What an odd reaction. Shouldn't he have been pleased? Wouldn't a man anxious to start a second marriage have been overjoyed to discover the barriers had already been dismantled? The tiny flame swelled and warmed. Ruark's attitude had been strange from the start. She recalled his comment that he thought if they had stayed together, they would have solved their problems.

Katrin was aglow. How blind she had been! Ruark could never have genuinely wanted a divorce or, if he had, seeing her again had swiftly changed his intention. No man, in love with another woman, could have devoted himself so fervently to pleasing her as he had done, less than

an hour ago. A stupid grin spread across her face.
Pride, that destructive pride Arlene had spoken
of, must have got in the way of him revealing his
true feelings. Katrin thought about her own
pride—the need to mask her hurt—and how it
had generated a glib bravado. Right from that
dreadful day when Ruark had packed his bags
and boarded the Hong Kong plane alone, she had
erected her optimistic façade.

'I was too young to marry,' she had tossed out
with a smile, 'but everyone's entitled to a trial
run.'

Her suffering had been camouflaged, never
spoken of, even to her father. *Especially* her
father. Felix had been fooled, though whether she
had so successfully fooled Oliver, she doubted.
Her single confidante and safety-valve had been
Arlene, and later this evening Arlene would be
dining with Ruark. Katrin's grin grew wider. Her
initial reaction when Ruark had revealed the
dinner date had been one of pique—why hadn't
Arlene told her? Now she understood. Her
friend must have guessed Ruark might wish to
take her into his confidence, and so had been
discreet. But Arlene cared about them both.
Nothing would please her more than to play
Cupid and push them into matrimony again.
Not that they had ever been out of matrimony,
but she wouldn't know that unless Ruark chose
to tell her. This evening everything would come
right. Arlene would make it right. 'Stretch out
a hand,' she had instructed. Katrin was convinced she would offer the very same advice to
Ruark.

Time passed, and by nine o'clock she was
twitchy. Presumably the dinner date was under-

way? Once her husband realised her love for him
was as strong as ever—for Arlene would be sure
to hint, if not make an outright declaration—
would he rush back here to stake his claim?
Maybe any moment now there would be a ring at
the door, and Ruark would be stood there? She
laughed at such wishful thinking. No matter what
Arlene revealed, he would never be so impolite as
to desert a companion mid-evening. But suppose
her friend prodded him to leave? Ruark might be
coming up in the lift this very minute, ready to
insist he spend the night with her, and all the
other nights for the rest of their lives. The
prospect made her pulses tingle.

Katrin told herself to be sensible. Ruark had
always been crazy over the barbequed seafood
served in the east coast's open-air restaurants
fifteen miles away, and if that was the
destination he would be unlikely to return to the
city until after midnight. How did she exist
until then? She decided to bake. Thanks to a
cookery course she had taken three months ago,
she could now rustle up everything from a
sponge cake to a meringue gâteau at the drop of
a hat.

Not exactly at the drop of a hat, Katrin
realised, when she opened the fridge door. The
last of the eggs had been scrambled for her
supper, and the sugar jar held little more than a
spoonful. So baking was out. Katrin cast
around for something else to occupy the time,
and suddenly remembered her father's old
writing case. Maybe she ought to read the
letters, despite them being sadly out of date,
just to check they contained nothing of importance? She retrieved the case from the

cardboard box in the broom cupboard, and sat
the envelopes in a pile beside her on the sofa.
One by one she read the letters, and one by one
they proved to be dull. Felix's friends had
written, elderly men who were obsessed with
the low level of company pensions, or their
gardens, or fishing holidays. Katrin was bund-
ling the correspondence back into the writing
case when she noticed a rip in the watered silk
lining. Something was tucked inside. She inserted two fingers and her violet eyes widened.
On a manilla envelope her father's name and
address were written in Ruark's big black
scrawl, and the postmark said Hong Kong.
With feverish haste, she found two sheets of
notepaper.

Dear Felix,
    After crawling through four of the un-
happiest weeks in my life, I am compelled to
write and beg you to send Katrin to me. You
alone can persuade her to cut loose, although
leaving will be difficult for her because the
two of you share a closeness which is to be
envied.
    I can't pretend that living here with me
won't be difficult for her, either. Although I'm
based in Hong Kong right now, the demands
of my career mean I continue to travel as
excessively as I did in Singapore. Katrin will
be on her own for days and nights on end. In
addition, I can't yet afford to lavish on her the
luxury she takes for granted at the big house.
Property prices are exorbitant here, so a
glorified bedsit, without servants! is the most I
can manage.

Recently I've been taking a critical look at myself, and at the past. I admit to rushing Katrin into marriage with very little serious thought as to how she would cope. I loved, and love, her passionately, and in my haste to make her mine, I imagined that would be sufficient. It isn't.

Because you (motivated by Oliver, no doubt) had that *idée-fixe* about us moving in with you after our honeymoon, I agreed. I was wrong. And yet if we had set up home in Singapore on our own, the temptation for her to rush back to you whenever I was away on business would have doubtless proved too strong to resist. That's why prising her from Singapore is vital. Yes, she'll hurt. Yes, she'll be miserable in the night when she's alone. But one day I shall stop travelling, one day I shall have enough money to indulge her.

I promised Katrin I would write, but on reflection I seem to have said all I have to say here. Would you pass this letter to her, please? I recognise (as I'm sure you do) that at times I'm too damned hasty for my own good. Taking my wife off for a week-end to talk things over would have made far more sense than issuing an ultimatum, but at the time I wasn't making much sense. I don't know if I am now!

Don't bother to reply. A telex to the office advising Katrin's flight number and arrival time will be answer enough! And if Oliver kicks up a fuss, for god's sake overrule him.

With heart in mouth.

                                                        Ruark

Katrin sagged. So he *had* written, had cared enough to give her a second chance! She didn't know how to react. Did she laugh, or cry, or yell a protest? Anyone reading the letter would presume he referred to some pampered darling, but she wasn't like that. Not now, a voice agreed inside her head, but think back. Had she really been so cosseted and cushioned? Maybe, maybe not. She pushed the two sheets of paper back into their envelope and frowned, wondering how valid Ruark's view of her had been. She did not know. But one thing she *did* know—he had not shown much insight where her relationship with her father was concerned.

In time she accepted Ruark was not going to appear on her doorstep, but she went to bed content. After the meal, Katrin had decided, he would have taken Arlene home and returned to his hotel room to think things through. Tonight he would be planning his strategy, for tomorrow he would be talking to her about their future. She drifted off to sleep, secure in the knowledge that if confirmation had been needed of his feelings for her, the letter had provided it. Ruark, too, had longed for them to be reunited. He, too, regretted the past. And if her father had shown her the letter, those fifteen months apart would never have happened.

'Aren't you going to tell me about your dinner date?' she asked the next morning, unable to bottle up her curiosity any longer. The half-hour since Arlene's arrival at the agency had been spent discussing the requirements of a peanut manufacturer's TV commercial, but time was passing. Soon they must leave for the Regent.

Soon, Katrin had no doubt, she would be seeing Ruark again. He would be champing at the bit, eager to claim her the minute the fashion show ended. But before that happened, she was desperate to hear the events of the previous evening. 'Where did you go? Was the food good?' She grinned, abandoning all pretence. 'All I need to know is, what did he say about us?'

Arlene ran a finger along the crease of her tomato-red slacks. 'Not much.'

'You didn't——'

'We didn't spend much time on personal chat. In any case, what happens between you and Ruark is your own affair. It's easier if I don't get drawn in.'

Deflated by this unexpected declaration, Katrin shrugged. She tried not to care, but when she spoke the chagrin was evident in her voice. 'Okay, so you played things light and easy. I suppose that's a fair comment.'

'Ruark asked me to give you this.' Arlene rummaged in her handbag to find an envelope. 'I expect he explains why he's gone.'

'Gone?'

'He's checked out of the Regent.'

'But he can't have gone,' Katrin protested, suddenly beset by demon fears. 'He can't have checked out.'

'Sorry, Kat, but he has.'

'When? Why? For how long? I mean, he is coming back isn't he? He must,' she wailed, her beautiful image of their reconciliation disappearing behind a fog of distress. She tore open the envelope, her eyes flying over the words he had written.

'Well?' asked Arlene, willing the note to solve everything. She hated seeing Katrin so upset.

'He needs to be alone for a few days. At least, I think that's what he says, his writing is terrible. At a guess, he wrote the letter with his head in a paper bag.' She stared numbly at the second paragraph, but baulked at revealing that particular message. 'Ruark reckons he'll return.'

'Then he will.'

'When, in fifteen months' time?' She dropped the letter disconsolately down on the desk.

'This needn't be history repeating itself.' Arlene rested a comforting hand on her arm. She paused, then said, 'Shouldn't you consider that Ruark may have a perfectly legitimate reason for disappearing?'

Her chin jerked up. 'You know where he's gone,' she accused.

'Well, yes,' Arlene admitted, a flush creeping up her throat. 'But he's asked me to keep his location a secret for now. I'm sorry, Kat, I feel awful about this, but——'

Her friend might be squirming, but Katrin was in no mood to be charitable and let her off the hook. 'But you won't tell me? His whereabouts are to remain confidential because he doesn't want me to get in touch?' she flared. The barely perceptive nod of the strawberry-blonde head was humiliating. 'He needn't have any fears on that score,' she declared. 'The last person on earth that I would chase after is damned Ruark Lencioni.'

Most of the bed clothes were on the floor the next morning, so much for sleeping like a statue! Katrin doubted if she had closed her eyes all

night. She had heard a distant church clock strike
every hour, on the hour. Midnight, one o'clock,
two, three and four. At four she had switched on
the bedside lamp and re-read Ruark's second
paragraph.

I promise I'll be back. But in the meantime
I'd be grateful if you would contact a reliable
solicitor, and set our divorce in motion. I'll do
whatever's necessary to expedite matters. I
realise this is painful, and I'm sorry, but it's for
the best in the long run, believe me.

She did not believe him. She could not
understand how he had joined himself to her,
body and soul, then subsequently rejected her, all
in the space of twenty-four hours. Had she
completely misread his feelings? Katrin recognised that Ruark had always exhibited a certain
detachment, that was his style. Even in the close-
knit, happy days of their marriage he had never
given all of himself, but some inner sense had
told her he had had given as much as he was
prepared to give to anyone. Ninety per cent of
Ruark was far preferable to a hundred per cent of
any other man, and she had been content with
that. But she was not content now. Five o'clock
found her in tears. By dawn she was dry-eyed
and desolate. Understanding his desertion was
beyond her.

She was wide awake when the alarm clock went
off at seven-thirty. Pivotelle was closed on
Saturdays, but she made a practice of going into
the office for an hour or two, using the
uninterrupted time to review the past week's
work and plan the next seven days. Katrin was
checking invoices at her desk when she heard

someone knocking on the outer door. She found
Arlene stood there, looking flustered.

'I've been awake all night,' her friend began.

'Me, too,' Katrin intervened. 'And if you now
intend to come clean and divulge where Ruark's
gone, back to Sydney or wherever, couldn't it
have kept until after the weekend? By Monday
perhaps I'll be able to make some sense out of
that man, but right now——' The waft of her
hands indicated utter confusion.

'I don't think it ought to wait,' Arlene said
determinedly, 'you see, he's gone again. That guy
of yours is worse than the Scarlet Pimpernel. I
suppose this puts the tennis gang reunion out to
grass.'

'What do you mean—again?' Katrin asked, as
Arlene headed for the office. Whatever she had
come to say was obviously going to get said. The
blonde had not made a special journey to the
agency just to remain mute. 'And he isn't my
guy, or maybe he is, legally if temporarily. We
aren't divorced,' Katrin revealed, with a flaccid
laugh. 'Not like we thought we were. At least,
like I thought we were. As far as Ruark was
concerned we'd never stopped being married, but
it turned out the solicitor was crooked.'

Arlene gazed at her, open-mouthed. She found
the nearest chair and sat down. 'Do you think
you could say all that again, and in slow motion?'

Katrin explained the entire débâcle. Lack of
sleep was doubtless responsible for her precarious
emotions, but at intervals during the tale tears
brimmed, while seconds later she was laughing at
her ridiculous plight.

'And the crazy thing is, we can't leave each
other alone. Twice we've——' She hesitated,

wondering if she was divulging too much, then decided Arlene would understand. 'Twice we've ended up making love. I was convinced we had a chance at a future together, but——' She clenched her teeth, on the verge of tears again. 'Ruark still wants a divorce. In the note you passed on, he asked me to consult a solicitor.' She sniffed hard. 'I still can't make any sense of him disappearing like he did.'

Arlene fidgeted with one of four gold bracelets which encircled her arm. 'He had no alternative. He was taken into hospital.'

'Hospital?' Now it was Katrin's turn to be open-mouthed.

'Barnaby's. He was there just for a couple of nights.'

There was relief at hearing his stay had been brief and that the hospital was a local one in Singapore, but the relief lasted only a moment.

'What's the matter with him?' she demanded.

'Eye trouble. On Thursday evening, when we met at the Regent for a drink, Ruark started having difficulty with his sight,' Arlene explained. 'One moment he was fine, the next he began blinking furiously.'

'He couldn't focus?'

'That's right. How did you guess?'

'Because the same thing happened once when we were together. How long did the attack last?'

The older woman sighed. 'That's the problem. Ruark assured me any lack of vision would correct itself in seconds, but several minutes passed by before he could see again. I'm afraid then I made rather a nuisance of myself. He was reluctant to break up our evening, but I wore him down.' She flashed Katrin a weak grin. 'Harridan that I am I insisted on driving him to the outpatients department at Barnaby's, and, purely by chance, the opthalmologist, or whatever you call him, was on hand. He did an examination and decreed Ruark must stay there for the night. Before I left, Ruark insisted on writing you a note, though at the time his vision was poor.'

'Hence the bad writing?'

'Yes.'

'And you didn't tell me?' Katrin flared, her voice hobbled with pain. She felt like sobbing out loud at the injustice of Arlene's deception. 'The man you know I love was lying in hospital, unable to see, and you kept quiet!'

The blonde started to offer a hasty explanation. 'Ruark said the problem would be cleared up at speed, and that there was no reason to worry you. That's why I agreed to do as he asked, and say nothing. Maybe he thinks he's being gallant, but he seems to have some cock-eyed idea about protecting you.'

'Protecting me!' she almost yelled. 'Why should I need protection? I'm twenty-five years old. I'm fully aware life isn't all beer and skittles.'

'That's what I told him. I said you could handle whatever came your way, that you were bullet-proof. But I'm afraid he didn't seem to believe me.'

'And now you say he's gone again? You mean he's left the hospital?'

'This morning,' Arlene confirmed. 'That's why I'm here. All along I've been uncomfortable about keeping quiet, but this new development was too much. I needed to see you and explain what's been happening.'

'How kind!'

'Please, don't be hurt. I understand how you feel, but Ruark did promise me he'd phone you in a day or two. I apologise.'

Katrin sighed, finding her anger difficult to sustain. Arlene was a good friend, and could hardly be blamed if she had been trapped between conflicting loyalties.

'Apology accepted. I know how persuasive Ruark can be when he puts his mind to it.' She changed tack. 'Do you have any idea what happened in hospital?'

'He underwent a series of tests. I visited him yesterday evening,' the blonde revealed, 'and he was in high spirits. He said he'd have the results of the tests today.' Arlene sighed. 'But when I rang earlier this morning to check on the state of play, a receptionist told me that he'd been discharged.'

'His vision problems have been solved?'

'I presume so. All the girl knew was that Ruark had gone off for a few days' rest. He'd managed to rent a holiday bungalow. She mentioned a long-distance taxi being booked to take him to Telok—something or other.'

'Telok Cinta.' Katrin swooped on the name, feeling it was a good omen. 'That's the little bay where we spent our honeymoon. It's on the east coast of Malaysia.'

'Far from Singapore?'

'Not really, about a three-hour drive.' Abruptly she grinned. 'I could drive there this afternoon and surprise him.'

Arlene looked dubious. 'Do you think that's wise?'

'To hell with wisdom, it's what I'm going to do!'

*   *   *

Even before Katrin's passport had been stamped by customs on the causeway which linked Singapore with Peninsula Malaysia, doubts were surfacing. She told herself lack of courage was responsible for weakening her resolve and that she must stick to her original decision. Yesterday she may have declared that Ruark was the last person on earth she would chase after, but hadn't she refused to follow him once before, with disasterous results? She wasn't going to make that mistake again.

She drove down the sun-baked main street of the Malaysian frontier town, and turned right on to the long straight highway which would eventually deposit her on the east coast. This road was well-tarred, passing through villages, palm oil plantations and mile upon mile of rubber trees, but once she neared Telok Cinta she must switch to what was little more than a beaten track through the jungle. The track was deeply rutted and dusty in the dry weather, a quagmire in the wet.

Fifty miles on, and Katrin's doubts had billowed and darkened like the clouds which had appeared on the horizon. Blue sky had now begun to give way to slate-grey cumuli, and the speed at which they were gathering meant a storm lay ahead. No doubt Ruark would storm when he discovered how Arlene had betrayed his trust! Another fifty miles nearer the secluded bay, and her idea of confronting him seemed more ill-conceived than ever. What foolish impulse had set her on this road? What had made her imagine the rock-throwing girl was of minor importance, and that Ruark might still love *her*?

Katrin began to wonder what she was going to

say when she arrived at the wooden bungalow which sat on a white-sand beach, overlooking the South China Sea. Would she bound across the verandah, walk into the airy living room and say casually, 'I heard you'd been in Barnaby's, and I thought I'd enquire how you are?'

Suppose he said, 'I'm fine. Thank you for calling,' and showed her the door. What did she do then? She had not thought that far ahead. In truth, she hadn't thought ahead at all. The idea of joining him at Telok Cinta had been so persuasive that she had locked up the Pivotelle suite, waved goodbye to Arlene and set off. All she had were the clothes she stood up in—a cutaway rose-violet cotton top and matching slacks—and her handbag, containing passport and sufficient petrol money.

The sky grew darker and darker. At the next charmingly lackadaisical village Katrin noticed shopkeepers bringing in wares from the roadside, and battening down shutters in preparation for bad weather. The storm was coming up faster than she had anticipated, and in the tropics, when it stormed, it stormed! Driving in heavy rain, with erratic thunder and lightning a background concerto, could be frightening. Katrin sighed. She was much closer now to Telok Cinta than Singapore, so the sensible way must be forward. Perhaps if she kept her foot down, she would reach the bungalow before the heavens opened?

Nearly there! she thought, as she swung the Ford on to the narrow track some three miles from the bay, but then she heard a low menacing rumble of thunder. On either side of the track thick dark green jungle stretched up like walls, turning an already gloomy day into night. Katrin switched on her headlights. The electricity which lay heavy in the hot stagnant air was making her head buzz, but she kept a relentless pressure on the accelerator. A jagged white-hot scar cracked across the sky, and she jumped. Seconds later, the rain came. Large dollops splattered on the dusty track, washed down the windscreen, rattled like pellets on the car roof. Another rumble, another ear-splitting sear of lightning, and the storm was overhead. Water slooshed down, as if by the bucketful, transforming the track into a mud canal in seconds. The windscreen wipers, flicking back and forth like insane fingers, were barely coping.

Through a blur of running water, Katrin saw what lay ahead. She went cold. She had quite forgotten about the bridge. Before she reached the bungalow, she had a stream to cross. At least, on her honeymoon there had been a stream, but now, to her dismay, she saw a river, a raging mud-brown river which swilled against the wooden planking. In the dry the half-a-dozen lengths of timber had been high above the water and had made an adequate bridge. But not now. Dare she drive over such a flimsy sodden structure in these conditions? Katrin wondered if she should turn back, but how could she turn back? If she slowed, the Ford would get bogged down in the mud which was spraying up on either side. Her only chance was to keep moving, and if she was to reach the other bank she must cross over at a fair lick. To stall midway would be catastrophic. Nerves held tightly in control, she pressed down her foot and increased her speed. The car hit the bridge with a crunch, she heard the planks creak and groan a protest.

'Steady girl,' she told herself, trying not to visualise the bare inches to spare on either side. 'Keep dead straight.'

After what seemed an age, but which could only have been seconds, the Ford lumbered off the planks on to the other bank. Katrin allowed herself a moment of congratulation—foolishly, for in that moment her foot eased, and the car sank axle deep in the mire. She accelerated, but all she achieved was flying mud and a sucking sound as the car wallowed. In despair, she switched off the ignition. What did she do now? Here she was, stuck in the pouring rain in the middle of nowhere, on a fool's errand, with thunder crashing about her and lightning crazing the sky.

Katrin folded her arms over the steering wheel and wearily rested her head. Chasing after Ruark was futile. Shouldn't she just do as he asked, arrange a divorce and call it quits? Okay, they had made love, and it had been beautiful, but making love was a physical thing. Sex wasn't necessarily an indication of love as far as a man was concerned. She may equate sex with love, and love with marriage, but Ruark thought differently. She knew he did. She had gone into her marriage bed a virgin, but he hadn't. He had made love to women before her, and doubtless since her, she thought despondently, but he had never been in love with them. Equally, because he had made love to her did not mean he *loved* her. She attracted him, Katrin acknowledged that, but——

A pounding on the side window, a yank at the

door handle made her heart jump in panic.
Someone was out there in the storm. As the door
was wrenched open she cowered back, the rain
stinging on her arms and face.

'What in hell's name are you doing here?'
Ruark demanded. Blue-black hair was plastered
across his brow. He was dripping wet, his shirt
like a rag, and furious. Grabbing her shoulder,
he virtually dragged her out of the car. 'Come
on, I suppose you'd better join me at the
bungalow.'

Trying to stay upright on the inches of mud
which squelched into her sandals, Katrin watched
as he switched off the headlights, removed the car
keys, and thrust her bag into her hands. Already
she was drenched.

'Run,' he commanded.

Between the car and the bungalow stretched a
grove of palm trees. Here the vegetation thinned
out, and as a high-intensity glare of lightning lit
the sky Katrin caught a glimpse of pounding grey
waves in the distance. Telok Cinta was no
tropical paradise today, it was a savage, wet hell.
A hand gripping her elbow, Ruark propelled her
through the trees. The earth was greasy, the rain
blinded, but he forced her along. Another bellow
of thunder, with its mean streak of lightning,
made her heart race. They were through the palm
trees and into a clearing. In the middle sat a small
wooden bungalow, one of three which were
discreetly sited around the bay.

One last final stretch, and he forced her up the
steps. Together they skidded across the wet
boards of the verandah and ended up in the living
room.

'How are your eyes?' Katrin panted.

He tried to catch his breath. 'You've never come all this way to ask me that?'

'Well—yes.' She didn't know what else to say. She shuffled her feet, shook a raindrop from the end of her nose, and heard the patter of rain on the roof.

'Dear God!' Ruark gave a strangled laugh. 'You refused to board a plane and fly in comfort to Hong Kong, yet now you drive alone through a tropical storm, risk being drowned in that jungle torrent out there, and just to enquire if my vision is twenty-twenty?'

'I was worried,' she said, and could not stop a shiver. The temperature might still be high, but her wet clothes were clinging, and the ceiling fan which circled above was reducing her body heat by the second. 'Arlene explained you'd had a couple of nights in Barnaby's and said there'd been tests. I—I wondered how you were.'

Ruark swept a hank of sodden black hair out of his eyes. 'You haven't arrived complete with grapes and the latest copy of *Playboy*, as well?'

Katrin wished she had never come. She was soaked through, cold and miserable. Ineffectually she attempted to dry her hands on her backside. He would think she was demented if she said the reason for this impetuous dash through Malaysia was because she harboured some mad fool hope about him still loving her. That maybe he did not want a divorce, even though he had said so, and that the Australian girl was merely a passing frolic? Now she recognised she was demented herself. Frowning, she saw that Ruark was prising off his muddy sports shoes.

'Would you do something for me?' she asked,

when he padded barefoot across the polished pine
floor to the window.

'What?'

His stance was tense, his eyes wary. Now she
had heart-stopping evidence of how much he
objected to her presence. Katrin supposed she
should have expected this—why else would he
have asked Arlene to keep his whereabouts a
secret?—but to actually see it for herself was
debilitating. She scowled at his abandoned shoes,
his footprints, and then up at him.

'Stop spreading mud around. Sling your shoes
out on to the verandah, they can't get any wetter
there, and don't lean against anything or sit
down, otherwise you'll mess up the bungalow.'

He laughed, and she heard his relief. 'I never
thought I'd hear you on the hausfrau kick,' he
commented, but did as she asked, stepping
carefully back across the room on the original
footprints to shovel his shoes outside the door.
He turned back to her. 'As soon as the rain stops,
you must leave. If it clears within the next half
hour you've a reasonable chance of reaching
Singapore before nightfall.'

Such iceberg ruthlessness took her breath
away. 'Must you push like this?' Katrin retaliated.
'I've driven flat out for three hours, covered
heaven knows how many miles, and you expect
me to turn right around and drive straight back?
You make a lousy host.'

Ruark took out a sodden handkerchief and
tried to dry his face. 'I don't intend to push, I
intend to be sensible. Between us we screwed
things up the last time, but I won't let that
happen again. The moment the rain steadies off is
the moment you head home.'

'Would you like me to leave right now?' she demanded hands on hips. 'What does it matter if I get struck by lightning or smashed to pulp by a falling tree? Good grief, I arrive bearing good wishes and what I find is you, welcoming as a shark, except you move faster! At least tell me what the hospital said.'

His tongue worried the corner of his mouth. 'My sight requires corrective treatment. An operation is scheduled for a week tomorrow.'

CHAPTER SIX

'An operation? What kind of operation?' she asked, her violet eyes as large as startled pansies.

'Magnetism.' Ruark saw her perplexity. 'It's an involved story, and before I explain I guess we'd both better get out of our wet clothes. You're right, I am being a lousy host. I don't want you to stay here, but that doesn't mean I insist you go down with pneumonia.' He touched her arm. 'You feel as if you're frozen through. A hot shower will remedy that. Is there a change of clothes in your car?'

''Fraid not.' Katrin's teeth were threatening to chatter, and she shivered. 'This visit was sheer impulse. I just leapt into the driving seat and drove.'

'Sounds more like me than you,' he said, with a wry raise of a brow. 'You go off to the bathroom, and while you're under the shower I'll see what I can rustle up for you to wear.'

Katrin stood beneath the hot water until she was warmed right through and when, at last, she opened the plastic curtains she found Ruark had deposited a navy sweater and pair of dark checked trousers by the door. His discretion struck her as edging on the comic. In the old days they had had no inhibitions, so pushing in dry clothes while she was hidden from view, without even a shout to tell her, smacked of the prudish. In the old days he would have poked in a hand to pat her rear, or pulled her out from beneath the water to kiss her, or even flung off his clothes and joined her. But these weren't the old days.

She towelled her hair, then bounced the damp curls through her fingers. Ruark's clothes were much too big, but he had provided a belt to keep the trousers aloft, and by dint of rolling up legs and sleeves, she managed to fashion a reasonable outfit. The prospect of joining him in the living room was a little rich for her blood, so she spent a minute or two more trying to jolly her tangled hair, and her spirits, back into life. She knew now that all she had been doing over the past few days was weaving a web of hopes, but webs, no matter how intricate or carefully constructed, are fragile things. Whatever cobweb alliance she had thought might entwine her and Ruark together had now disintegrated. He did not want her here. All she could do was wear a brave face, and shoot off to Mersing, a little fishing village some ten miles away, or even drive home to Singapore, as soon as the rain stopped.

'And here we have a sophisticated little number by Lencioni,' she announced, using an exaggerated mannequin's sway to enter the living room. 'Note the soft and fluid silhouette.'

'Baggy,' Ruark grinned, carrying two steaming mugs from the kitchen.

'Balanced by six-inch heels and fishnet tights.'

'Flat feet in my old socks. El Wrecko.'

She pouted. 'Thanks, but I can't win 'em all.'

'You win enough, pussycat. Even if your face does shine, and that topknot tells me you've been fighting orang-utans.'

'This is finger-combing,' she protested. 'Once my hair's dry it'll look fantastic.'

Ruark pulled a face.

He was the one who looked fantastic, Katrin thought, watching as he bent to place the mugs on a low rattan-and-glass table. He had changed into a grey sweatshirt and shorts, the kind of shorts guaranteed to make Arlene's, and any other woman's, palms itch. They fitted over his backside like a second skin, cut high to reveal firm tanned thighs, surfaced with black hair. She almost put out a hand to touch him herself, but decided if she did he would probably banish her from his sight with no more ado. The charmer who had so casually suggested 'a tumble in the hay' had disappeared. This Ruark would not pull her beneath him on to the sofa, nor coax her into a striptease. This Ruark had his sensuality under tight control. The time for lovemaking was over, other matters concerned him now. She wondered what was going on behind those blue eyes, those direct blue eyes which could not be as bright and healthy as they appeared.

'Tell me about the magnetism,' she said, when they were sipping their mugs of hot chocolate. 'Why is it necessary?'

'Because I have tiny particles of metal in my eyes. They're the reason I've been having difficulty in seeing.'

'How did they get there?' Katrin asked. 'And when?'

He tried to be offhand, but ended up giving a stiff kind of smile. 'At the time of the accident with Dick. The opthalmologist's theory is that when the cable broke and flicked across my face, minute pieces of metal sheared off. They must have mixed with the blood and somehow disappeared into my eyes.'

'But why should trouble flare up after all this time?'

'It seems that by some freak the particles had been lodged out of harm's way, but a sudden movement, maybe something as simple as a jerk of my head, has brought them back into circulation. Now fluids are acting on them to form chemical compounds, and the compounds have been responsible for my . . . black-outs.' She could tell he detested the word.

'How long have you been having these . . . black-outs?'

Ruark tugged at his nose. 'A few weeks. At first I was aware of a hotness, a grittiness, but nothing to kick up a fuss about. I thought I'd been overdoing the deskwork, that's all. I presumed that when I came to Singapore and had a break from reading and writing reports, matters would correct themselves. But they didn't. Yet, until Thursday evening, any black-outs have been transitory, lasting seconds. On that occasion the seconds stretched into minutes. Dear God! the time seemed like eternity. I got one hell of a fright.' He sucked in a reflective breath. 'I can't stop imagining what could have happened if I'd been behind the wheel of a car at the time.'

'Were you in pain?'

'No, just a blue funk!'

'And a week tomorrow, these particles are to be removed by being magnetised?'

'That's it. I have drops which the doctor says will hold things in abeyance until next Sunday, so there's no immediate danger.'

Katrin drained her mug. 'But why wait until next Sunday? Is there some reason why he's not doing the magnetism immediately?'

'I asked for a stay of execution.'

'Why?' she asked cautiously, not caring for his choice of phrase. Ruark was keeping something from her.

'Because I need time to come to terms with the implications.'

The set of his jaw warned her Ruark was not about to lavish details, so she decided a little roundabout probing was necessary.

'I imagine removing the particles isn't quite as simple as picking pins from a carpet?'

His grin switched on and off. 'You imagine right. The doctor has an electro-magnet, which is a sophisticated piece of technology, and he's going to draw the foreign bodies from the deeper part of my eyes into the anterior chamber. Then they can be plucked out.'

Katrin watched him closely. 'Is success guaranteed?'

He pushed his hands into the pockets of his shorts, and stared at the door. 'In my case, the success rate is said to be around fifty per cent.'

'And what happens if the magnetism doesn't work?' she asked, making sure her tone remained neutral.

Ruark refused to look at her. 'Damn Arlene,' he muttered. 'Damn her to hell. Why did she have to blab about me going into Barnaby's?'

'You'd rather cope with this alone?' she flared, stung by his protest.

'Yes, yes I would!' he shot back. 'And don't look so . . . wounded.'

'Wounded!' She tossed off a laugh. 'I'm not wounded, I'm disembowelled. Do you know what it feels like to be rejected like this when I——'

She could not bring herself to tell him she loved

him, that was too sensitive a hurdle to jump in the circumstances. 'When I want to help, when I want to share?' she continued. 'All we shared in the past were the good times. When the bad times came, we split up. That was wrong.' Katrin lost patience with herself. Analysing their marriage was pointless. 'So, what happens if the magnetism doesn't work?' she repeated.

'Nobody quite knows. If the metal remains *in situ* there's the danger of a destructive inflammation occurring spontaneously.'

'Destructive?'

He raked a hand through his hair. 'I could end up with partial vision.'

'Partial?'

'Would you kindly stop extracting words and jabbing them back under my nose?'

'Yes, if you'd kindly stop being a schlep,' she retorted, sweet as pie.

'Okay.' Ruark made a gesture of resignation. 'Partial means I'll possibly need to give up the advertising world and stop driving cars, things like that. And here the word to extract is "possibly" because that's what all this is, just a possibility.'

'But a possibility you're considering?'

'It would be foolish not to. I need to consider the whole rigamarole before it lands in my lap as a *fait accompli*.'

'Hence the postponement of the magnetism?'

'Yes.' He was staring at the floor again. 'If things go . . . wrong, chances are I'm not likely to be sturdy as far as emotions go for a while. That's why it's vital I plan now. I must know exactly which path to take, given the various options.'

'That sounds rather coldblooded, and selfish.'

He lifted his head. 'Selfish?'

'Certainly. You don't live in a vacuum, Ruark, none of us do. Your future affects others. What about the rock-throwing girl, isn't she to be consulted?'

He looked at her for a moment. 'You can't be serious?'

'Yes, I am serious,' Katrin said hotly. 'Keeping her in ignorance is wrong. It's your duty to talk to her and explain what's involved. We never talked, that was our problem. Don't commit the same error twice.'

To her surprise, he hooted with laughter. 'But the rock-throwing Sheila doesn't exist.'

'What do you mean?'

'She was a joke.'

'A joke!' Did he know he had cut the earth from under her? Katrin tried to find something solid to attach herself to. 'It was a very stupid joke,' she said primly.

'You must know I'd never fancy a big butch woman.'

'I know nothing of the sort.'

'You do now,' he grinned.

She accomplished a rapid reappraisal of the situation. 'But if you were joking, why did you say you were getting married again?'

'I didn't. You jumped to the conclusion, and I guess I played along because it seemed the easiest thing to do. The rock-throwing Sheila came straight off the top of my head. I was certain you'd tumble it. You, of anyone, should realise I like my women one hundred per cent feminine.'

His amusement at her expense irritated. Katrin needed to retaliate.

'I realise you like your women not wearing any underwear,' she shot back.

That sobered him in an instant. The sharp glance he gave said he knew darn well she was naked beneath the checked pants and sweater. Ruark rose from his chair.

'The rain seems to be easing off,' he said, looking out of the window.

Judging from the ceaseless thrum on the roof, that seemed doubtful, but Katrin didn't much care about the weather any more. All she could think about was what a fiend he had been, deceiving her like that.

'Great,' she trilled. 'Give me a couple of seconds and I'll throw on my wet clothes and motor three hours across Malaysia again.'

'I didn't mean that.'

'Oh no?'

'No. It's true I don't want you to spend the night here at the bungalow, but maybe you could find a room at the Mersing rest house? I'd be happier if you did. Don't drive back to Singapore today. The storm's bound to have uprooted trees and washed out pot holes, so the journey could be dangerous.' He walked over to her. 'How can I explain?' he sighed. 'Your presence here—well, I'm frightened it'll cloud the issues, and right now I need to think straight. I need to be objective, and act with my head, not my heart. And especially not with my hormones!'

'Do you?'

His gaze was grave. 'A moment ago you accused me of being selfish, but it seems to me that if I make an emotional decision, rather than a level-headed one, that really would be selfish.' He dropped down to sit beside her, and took hold of her hand. 'I'd rather we didn't spend the night together,' he coaxed, his thumb trailing a circle on her palm.

'Will your company pay for your hospitalisation?'

Such an abrupt switch of conversation made him smile. 'No, why should they? I'm here on holiday. Though it's been one hell of a holiday so far,' he said, a dark brow quirking.

'Barnaby's won't come cheap,' Katrin warned.

'I know that.'

'I'll chip in, Ruark,' she offered earnestly. 'My bank account's strong and——'

He squeezed her fingers. 'Thanks for the offer, pussycat, but I can manage to pay my own way in the world.'

She did not intend to tread on any toes, but her need to help him took precedence. 'Look, fifteen months ago your salary was modest, we both know that. I realise things have changed since then, but Barnaby's is a luxury private hospital. A stay of only a couple of days can be expensive, and the services of an opthalmologist for your operation will——'

'Things *have* changed,' he told her. 'What's made the biggest difference is that I'm not supporting Suzi and her boys any longer. She's found herself a well-paid job, managing a boutique.'

'You supported them?' Katrin was taken aback by this revelation. 'I never knew.'

'The insurance money she received after Dick was killed turned out to be a pittance, and although I gave her my share when I sold the boat, that was soon swallowed up. I couldn't stand by and see Dick's widow and kids go short.

Suzi suggested she put the boys in a day nursery and return to work, but they were only toddlers at the time. They were too young to be farmed out.' Ruark smiled and spread his hands. 'Now they're both at school and Suzi's employed, paying her own way, so everyone's happy.'

'But why didn't you tell me you supported them?' she challenged, cut to the quick at having been excluded from his confidence.

'Because I don't believe in distributing largesse, then broadcasting the news and basking in my own glory.'

Katrin digested this. 'Like Oliver?' she suggested.

Her stepbrother had taken great pleasure in spreading the word about his involvement in Pivotelle, always with an oblique hint about his generosity.

'Maybe. And, to be honest, he was another reason why I kept quiet. I didn't relish the idea of either him, or Felix, being allowed access into my private affairs.'

'But I would never have told them.'

His eyes flashed a metallic blue. 'No? The three of you were like some kind of Mafia.'

Katrin sensed a gap of something unsaid, and she made an instinctive jump. 'And you felt excluded?'

'Yes, I damn well did!'

The idea was so entirely novel that she just stared, then came a glimmer of how her relationship with her father and Oliver must have appeared to him.

'If only you'd told me you felt this way,' she protested.

'I did, but you never listened.' His shoulders

moved dismissively. 'To get back to your original offer. Thanks again, but I can finance my own hospital bills.'

Katrin tilted her head and listened. This time the noise of rain on the roof had definitely slackened, and there had been no thunder roll or flashes of lightning for several minutes.

'The storm seems to have passed,' she announced. 'I'll be on my way. I'll spend the night in Mersing. Can I keep your gear for now? I'll have my own clothes dried at the rest house, and drop your sweater and pants off on my way back to Singapore tomorrow.'

'Won't the other guests get rather a shock when you roll up looking like a bag lady?' he teased.

'Maybe, but I'll just swear I shrank in the rain.'

Ruark laughed. 'There's no need to rush off just yet,' he suggested hesitantly. 'Wait until the rain stops completely. You should even join me for dinner. I had the taxi driver stop in Mersing while I bought a load of provisions,' he explained. 'I can easily knock us up a salad.'

'No thanks. It'll be dark in an hour or so, and I'd rather not be on the road then. Just in case any branches have been blown down,' she explained. 'I'll wait another ten minutes, and then perhaps you'd give me a hand to push the car out of the mud?'

'Will do. How's Pivotelle progressing these days?' he asked conversationally.

'Thriving. Profits increase every year.'

He gave a sidelong glance. 'You don't sound ecstatic. Is that because Ollie runs the show?'

'He doesn't.' She saw his disbelief. 'Oh, as

usual he insists on making noises off, and talking
about how well *we're* doing, but the truth is that
he contributes nothing to the day-to-day organ-
isation of the agency. He attempts to project
himself as the big boss, but he's going to receive a
nasty shock when he returns from Antwerp.'

Ruark looked curious. 'In what way?'

'I've paid back his loan in full, plus interest,'
Katrin added sparkily. 'Which means he doesn't
have a foot in the door any longer. I intend to
inform him he's *persona non grata*. I'm sick and
tired of him interfering.'

'Wow!' he exclaimed, with something border-
ing on admiration. 'You appear to be taking your
life by the scruff of the neck and giving it a damn
good shake.'

'That's one way of putting it.'

How she wished she could take Ruark by the
scruff of the neck and shake *him*. If there was
no other woman in his life, why must she be
held at bay? Katrin felt as if he had dropped
her down in the centre of a vast emotional no
man's land, where the only roads led to pain
and longing.

'If the profits are increasing at Pivotelle, why
aren't you satisfied?' he enquired, and she
straightened her shoulders.

'Because I don't consider running a model
agency to be the summit of my ambitions,' she
pronounced, acting a trifle flip. 'Singapore is
such a tiny island that although Pivotelle is a
success, at best it's only a fair-sized fish in
nothing much more than a puddle. A wider
environment would be more challenging.'

'Like Australia?' he suggested.

'I was thinking more in terms of London or

New York,' she said quickly, needing to
separate her future from his, because wasn't
that the way *he* wanted it? 'And the rain's
stopped now.'

CHAPTER SEVEN

A BENEVOLENT sun smiled down. Past furies regretted, the heavens were now on their best behaviour, hopeful they might wheedle a way back into favour. Fat droplets of water collected, trickled, dripped among the fresh-washed greenery. The world glistened. A warm breeze stirred the branches of lacey casuarinas, creating miniature waterfalls. After rain, the tropics are vivid. The sky was azure blue, and the white sand shore shimmered like diamond floss.

Together they crossed the clearing. Beneath the palm trees the earth was beginning to steam, and they stepped through vapour, tinted gold by the sunshine, which rose and curled around their ankles like fairy-tale mist.

'Oh heavens! I never realised I'd driven into the middle of a bog,' Katrin exclaimed, when they reached the car.

'Well, you did,' Ruark retorted, in a voice which said the action was typical of her dimwitted ways. Grim-faced, he stalked around to investigate the Ford which was resting in sticky brown mud, looking as at home as any hippo. 'You won't have any joy revving up. Release the hand brake and I'll have a shot at pushing you on to firmer ground.' She was sliding into the driver's seat to do as she was told, when there was a violent burst of bad language. 'Don't bother,' he commanded, poking his head in the door.

'Why not?'

'Because the damn bridge has been swept away. You're going nowhere!'

Ruark strode off to the river bank, and Katrin followed behind. Not a single plank remained. No doubt they were tangled up in the under-growth somewhere, or floating happily on the South China Sea. So how could she cross the six-foot gap? The water, though calmer now, was deep; the flow swift and dedicated, carrying along a riffraff of vegetation loosened by the storm.

Ruark scowled, searching for possibilities, then heaved a fractious sigh. She knew he was about to raise hell.

'Don't panic,' she said quickly. 'The car might be going nowhere, but I am. Upstream's bound to be narrower and——'

'And you can make a flying leap to the other side?' he asked, full of scorn.

Her chin peaked. 'I can try.'

'And then what? You walk the ten miles to Mersing, some of it through thick jungle, most of it in the dark?'

'Wrong. I walk three miles to the road before the sun sets, and I flag down a taxi.'

'No way.' He flung her a barbed-wire look. 'You'll have to spend the night at the bungalow. You can take the bedroom and I'll stretch out on the folding settee in the living room. Perfectly safe.'

'For me, or you?' Katrin enquired, the knowledge that he found her presence so abhorrent freezing the words solid.

'*Me.*' He managed to procure a laugh from somewhere, though a harsh one. 'Amazing, isn't it? Earlier in the week I was obsessed with getting you into bed, but now my obsession is keeping you out.'

'Because you don't want those issues of yours clouded?' she asked, and when he gave a curt nod Katrin felt toothached.

'Maybe one of the other bungalows is free?' she suggested coldly. 'I could use that.'

'They're both unoccupied, but they're also locked and bolted. And I don't intend to indulge in a spot of breaking and entering on your behalf.'

They turned to tramp back to the bungalow. She did not know why, when Ruark was being so bloody-minded, but she needed to make amends.

'I'll make dinner,' she offered. 'Maybe I can come up with something more ambitious than salad.'

Much to her relief, she did. At least the meal was a credit to her, Katrin thought, if nothing else was. Her husband had always been an adventurous shopper, buying anything which tickled his taste buds, and when she discovered fresh seafood among the provisions, she made a garlic prawn dish which incorporated diced pineapple and cucumber, and was served with a bowl of fluffy white rice.

'Who taught you how to prepare this?' he asked, secretly delighting her when he helped himself to more. 'Ah Lan?'

She shook her head. 'I enrolled for a series of lessons.'

'So garlic prawns aren't the only arrow in your quiver?' he said, allowing her a gift, a grin.

'Good grief, no! I do a magnificent horseradish sherbert, and my devilled lobster bisque would

have tempted Wellington away from Waterloo,'
she replied, laughter in her violet eyes.

'You don't wash-up as well, do you?'

'You're speaking to a person who gained a
black belt in washing-up!'

'Then I'll dry.'

From then on, Ruark was prepared to be
merry, but although the merriment was sustained,
by ten o'clock Katrin had had enough. At heart
she did not feel merry, and suspected neither did
he. Pleading tiredness, she went off to bed. What
a wasted evening, she thought as she cleaned her
teeth with his toothbrush. After dinner, and the
shared washing-up, they had strolled barefoot
along the beach, still joking, still being determinedly superficial. The tropical night air had
been warm and caressing, fireflies had danced in
the darkness, stars had twinkled high above. A
background rhythm had been established by the
gentle roll of the surf. Yet, despite walking side
by side, Ruark had made certain they never
touched, even an accidental brush of the shoulder
being forbidden. And he had kept noticeably
clear of any reference to their honeymoon, when
such strolls had had a habit of ending up with
them entwined on the sand.

Katrin had been in bed mere minutes when the
patter of rain started on the roof. She gave a
tortured groan. Further rain was the last thing
she required. Come what may, she was determined to leave tomorrow. Even if the stream had
swollen to Amazon proportions by morning, she
would get across—by swimming if need be! She
could not spend another day with Ruark, not
with this 'hands off' routine of his to shrivel her
up. The rain grew heavier, bouncing like

ballbearings on a tin plate. First Katrin lay on
one side, and then on the other. Last night she
had had precious little rest and she felt dog-tired,
but how could she sleep with that noise?
Grabbing the pillow, she pummelled it around
her ears, and promptly discovered one end was
sopping wet.

'How did that happen?' she wondered out loud.
The drop of water which splashed on to her brow
provided the answer.

Katrin leapt out of bed and switched on the
light. Looking up, she discovered a damp patch
on the ceiling. A container was needed to catch
the drip-drip-drip, and fast. She pushed up the
sleeves of Ruark's plaid shirt which she had
requisitioned as a nightgown, then padded into
the kitchen. Katrin was on her knees, searching
in the cupboard beneath the sink, when she heard
footsteps behind her.

'Is there a bucket anywhere?' she asked. 'The
rain's coming in and the bed's getting soaked.'

'No bucket, but couldn't you use the washing-
up bowl?' he suggested. Ruark yawned, gave her
a bleary smile, and hitched up his blue-and-white
striped pyjama trousers. Katrin felt like making
an acid comment about the trousers, for in the
past he had always slept naked. She suspected he
was using them as some form of chastity belt,
frightened she might jump on him! She glared at
the trousers, and up at him, but he never noticed.
Instead he yawned again. 'When you've done
that, do you think you could put in my eye drops?
I forgot them.'

'Okay.' She grabbed the washing-up bowl. 'Go
back to bed. I'll be with you in a minute.'

The divan was attached to the wall and could

not be moved, so there seemed no alternative but to site the bowl where her pillow had been. She inspected the ceiling, and once she was satisfied there were no further damp patches or drips, she marched into the living room.

Ruark was laid flat on his back, eyes closed, the blue-black hair rumpled across his brow. He had dozed off. Katrin's irritation with him dissolved in seconds. He looked like a boy when he was asleep—a darling boy. The wave of tenderness which engulfed her meant she had to fight the impulse to bend and kiss him, to push the hair out of his eyes. His eyes! Abruptly the prospect of Ruark with damaged eyesight billowed. She felt the prick of tears and swallowed hard.

'Have you got the eyedrops?' he mumbled, coming awake.

She became as efficient as a night nurse, finding the phial, inserting two drops in each eye, providing a handkerchief. Duty done, she crossed to the door and switched off the light.

'Sleep well.'

'Don't go.' Ruark's low voice came out of the darkness, and halted her. She heard the patter of the rain, but also the pitter-patter of her own heart. 'Your bed's wet. You can sleep in here, with me. Just sleep. No ... nothing else.' He moved, stretching out a hand. 'I'd appreciate your company.'

Katrin stood there, undecided, her thoughts in a miserable tangle, then she walked to the bed-settee and climbed in beside him. He moved to make room, his arm automatically going around her shoulders as it had done so many times in the past. Ruark's personal thermostat had always been set a few degrees higher than hers, and now his body heat warmed her, burned her, set her aflame. She knew if he started to make love to her she would have no resistance, although she must come away angry and hurt. Their passion would knock her down, but for the moment she did not care.

They lay silently, side by side in the darkness, and after a few minutes she acknowledged Ruark had meant what he had said. Those issues were not going to be clouded! She did not know whether to feel grateful or disappointed.

Just when the even rhythm of his breathing had convinced her he was on the brink of sleep, he spoke.

'Do you ever dream about me?' he asked.

'Sometimes,' Katrin admitted, finding it easier to be honest in the darkness. She was grateful he could not see her face clearly, and read the desolation she knew must be written there.

'I've dreamed about you—often.' He sounded pensive. 'I managed to cope with the days, but at night everything used to fall to pieces. I had a spell when I soaked myself in booze in an attempt to keep from seeing your face every time I closed my eyes, but alcohol doesn't change much.'

Why must he say these things? Katrin lay immobile. He was feeding her fantasies again— the fantasy of him loving her, the fantasy of him not really wanting a divorce.

'This is double Dutch,' she accused, when silence followed. 'You lie here and tell me how much our separation upset you, and yet you came back to Singapore expressly to ask for a divorce? And, what's more, after all the brouhaha with Beng you're still anxious to——' She remembered the wording of his note. '—To expedite matters.'

'Things are different now.'

She waited for a fuller explanation, but none came. Katrin was forced into taking the initiative again. 'You're still talking double Dutch,' she insisted. 'I can't believe you came back with the intention of splitting us up finally. I think——' She lost her nerve.

Ruark stretched a muscled arm around her as though he was protecting her. 'What do you think, pussycat?'

'I think you're a gigantic paradox,' she complained, despising herself for ducking the issue.

'Am I? I suppose that's how I must appear.' She heard him sigh. 'Okay, you want the truth, I'll give you the truth. I did come back to try and mend our marriage. My sole aim was to get us back together again.'

'Yes?' She had tried to sound disdainful, but a silly little giggle emerged.

'I know I went an odd way about a reconciliation,' he agreed, 'but the thing was, coming across you so unexpectedly threw me in total. I had a plan worked out in my head—how I would wine and dine you, buy flowers, ply you with the memories of the past, the good memories. I saw us hidden away from the rest of the world in some shadowy corner, with soft lights. We would be relaxed in each other's company, and we would talk. I was going to be calm and sensible. I was going to charm the socks off you.'

'Only the socks?'

He laughed and bent to kiss her shoulder, his lips warm through the cotton shirt. 'No, not only the socks.' He raised his head and became serious again. 'I intended to stress the positive aspects of our marriage, and suggest we start again. I was geared up to wheedle and coax, do whatever it took, but this was based on me controlling the show, you understand? Instead —wham!—I walk into a restaurant in broad daylight and the voice which comes over the microphone is yours. You were the up-to-the-minute girl in those sexy leather trousers. You were so sharp, so composed and confident. Quite different from the Katrin I'd imagined. I guess I sort of went to pieces. Somehow I couldn't make myself say all the stuff I'd rehearsed. You seemed determined to avoid me, and because I was terrified of letting you go out of my life again, some upside down reasoning made me mention divorce. I almost felt it was expected of me. But my idea was that once we were pushed together to sort out the details, I'd find the right opportunity to say my set piece. The shadowy corner would materialise. But——' He broke off, leaving Katrin to wonder what emotions directed him. 'But then you told me we were already divorced. Dear God! everything went haywire.'

She stared up into the darkness, daring to hope.

'You never wanted a genuine divorce?' she asked.

'Not then.'

She shut her eyes tight. 'And now?' she said carefully.

'Like I said, now things are different.'

Thud, down she toppled. 'But why?' All of a sudden Katrin understood. 'Because of your eyesight!'

'Of course. You're a girl who deserves to take great big chunks out of life, not little nibbles.'

'What on earth are you talking about?'

'Nothing.' Ruark stirred restlessly. 'Let's not get involved in any discussions now. We can talk . . . later.'

'How much later?' she demanded.

'After a week Sunday. Let's wait until then.'

She disentangled herself from his arms and reached across to switch on a lamp. 'I don't want to wait,' she said, when she could see him. Katrin propped herself up on the pillows. 'I want to talk now. And, for a start, I want to know why you're in such a hurry to have me consult a solicitor.'

With mumblings of mutiny, Ruark pushed himself upright, too. 'That note was written at a very bleak moment,' he said grudgingly. 'My eyesight had zeroed at the Regent, and then when I reached Barnaby's I had another black-out. If you must know, I was terrified I was going to go blind.'

'So you decided to cut me loose?' she asked in amazement.

'That was the general idea.'

She stared at him, and suddenly his reasoning became crystal-clear.

'And now you're hedging your bets?' she accused. 'You intend to devote this week to working out two versions of the future? By next Sunday there'll be one set of actions ready and waiting for if the magnetism works, and another set for if it doesn't?'

'You're getting the gist,' he retaliated, picking up her anger and using it himself.

'Just give me a minute to work this out.' Katrin glared at him. 'You intend to go ahead with a divorce if your sight is damaged, but you'll grant permission for us to join forces again as Mr and Mrs Lencioni if you're in perfect working order?'

'I wouldn't have phrased things exactly like that, but——' He shrugged acceptance of her statement.

She gave a barbed laugh. 'I don't believe it!'

'Why not?' he asked, his tone emotionless.

'Because it's so sickeningly sacrificial, that's why.'

Ruark climbed out of bed and frowned down at her, the jut of his jaw reminiscent of Mount Rushmore. 'I'm being realistic, Kat,' he said.

'No, you're not. You know darn well that even if your eyesight does deteriorate, you won't go under. You're not the type. Admittedly it would be a raw deal and there'd be bad times, but you'd manage. You'd keep fighting.'

'I expect so,' he said impatiently.

Reckless warmth made her desert the bed and join him.

'I'd be there to help,' Katrin said, caressing his arm where the dragon writhed. 'I love you and—and I get the impression you love me?'

He ignored her tentative question, asking another instead. 'And love conquers all?' he demanded abrasively. 'But it doesn't, our past is proof of that. I'm sure we both loved each other fifteen months ago, and yet our marriage split. Given the strains and stresses which are bound to exist if my sight's impaired, it would split again.'

'You're wrong!' she cried, gripping his arm tightly, her nails biting in her desire to make him understand. 'We're both different people now—steadier, wiser.'

'Not that different,' he rasped.

'We *are*. And I wish you'd cut out the heroics, they don't suit you.'

'I'm not being heroic.' Ruark stepped back to break the contact. 'I don't know how to say this without it sounding insulting, but it seems to be the only way I can get through to you. You're a hot-house plant, Katrin. You've grown up in a fluffy pink world. All your life you've left the nitty-gritty to servants.' He raised a hand to stop her protest. 'I'm not criticising, I'm stating fact. In addition Felix hugged you so tightly that you've never gone short emotionally, either. You take security, emotional and material, for granted. When Oliver came into your life, that security was reinforced. Okay, Ollie isn't my favourite guy, but in his own way he loves you. He'd never refuse you anything. You know he's there if you need help.'

'But I don't want his help! I'm independent of him now,' she interjected.

'I accept that, but it still doesn't alter the fact that you've never known a single moment of hardship.' He touched the corner of his mouth with his tongue. 'If my sight deteriorates beyond a certain point, there'll be hardship. I'll be forced to resign from the advertising agency and my income will drop like a stone. Maybe there'll be the added drain of doctor's bills? Months, even years, of treatment? I don't know.'

He had given her a bodyblow. 'And you think I wouldn't be able to cope?' she gasped.

'There again, I don't know. But I have no intention of putting you in a position where you'll have to find out. I don't *want* you to find out. You have higher expectations than being Girl Friday to a guy who can't see properly. You deserve something better.'

Katrin's heart contracted with pain. 'I don't deserve anything,' she flared. 'I just want you and me to be together.'

'There's a fifty per cent chance of us being together, pussycat,' he soothed, and she saw from the smile he gave that he was anxious to lower the temperature. 'We're being too negative. The success of the magnetism will solve all our problems.'

Her eyes flashed. 'Oh no! Phony divorce apart, I did originally marry you for better or worse, for richer or poorer, in sickness or in health. You can't rewrite the rules at this late stage, Ruark. You might consider me a fair-weather bride, but I'm not. And I'm not prepared to discuss terms.' The lump in her throat was making speech difficult. 'You make all the plans you want over the next few days, but if the fifty per cent chance of the magnetism being successful comes off, don't bother to knock on my door.'

He twitched, as though she had thrown a bucket of cold water over him. 'You can't mean you'll only agree to stay married to me if my eyesight fails?' he asked incredulously.

'Can't I?'

'But that's ridiculous.'

'No more ridiculous than you intending to stay married on the proviso your eyes are fine,' she retaliated.

Ruark folded his arms. 'If this is some way of getting me over a barrel, Katrin, it's not going to work.'

'No barrel.'

Narrowed blue eyes raked over her. 'Then I guess we've reached stalemate?' he said.

'If you're not prepared to change your mind before the operation, yes.'

'I won't change,' he said stubbornly. 'I'm not dragging you down with me. I've begun to analyse the situation and——'

'Analyse!' Her laugh was bitter. 'That's typical. A part of you always did stand back and analyse our relationship. You could never bear to fling yourself into the deep end, and to hell with the consequences, could you? Isn't there some quote about caring, but never caring too much? Well, that's your creed, Ruark,' she declared.

He chose to skate over her tirade. 'Try to imagine how restricted your life would be, burdened with a husband who couldn't fulfil his proper role. What you want——'

'Correction. What you want for me. And you're wrong. I was married believing you to be as poor as a church mouse so, as far as finance goes, what would be different?' She thought she detected a flicker of indecision in him, and pressed on. 'I accept I've grown up in the lap of luxury, but I've never craved luxury. In fact, you're the one who burns with ambition. You're the man who worked every hour God sent, determined to make a success of his career. And why?' Katrin paused for breath. 'Because success equals wealth. And why is wealth important? Because when you were a kid, your family was so poor you had newspaper in your shoes to keep out the rain, and you swore one day you'd lick the world at its own game by becoming a rich man.' She flicked a hand. 'I don't have that hang-up.'

Ruark said nothing. She had a long list of other arguments ready assembled, but suddenly could see no point in continuing. It was late. She was weary. And why waste her breath on a mule-stubborn individual who would go his own way, no matter what she said or did?

'I'm off to bed,' Katrin announced, and this time he let her go.

By lying top to tail, she managed to find enough bed to rest on. Surprisingly, she dropped straight away into a deep, dreamless sleep, and felt much sturdier when she awoke next morning. The sun was shining, so Katrin washed her soaked clothes, together with Ruark's, and pegged them out to dry on a makeshift line. The rain in the night must have been brief, for the earth was firm and the mud was beginning to harden around the car.

After breakfast, calls from the river bank alerted them to the arrival of Malim, a local Malay who supervised the bungalows. After the matter of bridge-building had been discussed he disappeared, returning later with two friends and a fresh supply of timber. By noon the planks were in place and Katrin, clad once again in her own clothes, was able to leave. It was a toss-up whether she, or Ruark, was the most relieved at her departure. Words, apart from discussing practical matters, had been kept to a minimum. No plans had been made for them to meet again. Neither the divorce, nor Ruark's eyesight, had been mentioned. For now, it seemed, everything that could be said, had been said.

CHAPTER EIGHT

OVER the next week, Katrin became increasingly grateful for the demands of the fashion shows. They were lifesavers, a discipline which broke up her day and broke into her tendency to dwell on Ruark and matters concerning him. Of course Arlene had been eager to hear about the visit to Telok Cinta, but she had fashioned an evasive tale. Personal problems had been censored. Instead, she had explained the history of her husband's precarious eyesight, and hoped that Arlene would attribute her restless state entirely to worries about the operation.

But as the weekend approached the tentacles of her restlessness ranged and clawed ever wider. When was Ruark scheduled to return to Singapore? Would he get in touch? Maybe his time alone at the bungalow had brought about a change of mind? Or maybe not. Definitely not, she thought in despair. Ruark was too stubborn an individual to waver in any resolve. He had not wavered when the slashing cable had sliced between him and Dick. He had not wavered when their separation had made alcohol a temporary retreat. And now he would not waver in his determination to set her free, should his future look bleak.

By Friday, after five nights when her mind had spun and sleep had been intermittent at best, Katrin was as highly strung as a taut bow. Maybe Ruark was back in town, already installed at

Barnaby's? Every time the phone rang, her nerves leapt. Every time she heard a heavy footstep or a masculine voice, her heart thudded. But she had no news of him.

That night, as she lay in bed, her mind started on its familiar revolutions. All week she had been aware of ever-decreasing circles, and now her thoughts fused into one stark immovable fact— she loved him too much to leave him of her own accord. No matter how bruised her ego was at being regarded as a rare and useless orchid, she would agree to do whatever Ruark asked. When the crunch came, she would let him walk all over her. Pride was a thing of the past. Her command that he should not come knocking on her door was recognised as sabre-rattling. She accepted that she would fly to his side if he so much as crooked a finger. Her eyes filled with tears. Ruark's finger would only crook if the magnetism was successful—so everything hinged on the operation!

Saturday dawned, bright and sunny. As she drew back the curtains, Katrin thanked providence that today was so jam-packed she'd have little time for morbidly reviewing her private life. Once she had eaten breakfast she was off to Pivotelle, but a shorter visit than usual. Errol, the hair show choreographer, had been in touch, so she had to report to the Regent's ballroom before noon. Errol was an excitable young Malay, full of neoteric ideas, and when she had heard his views on the show, she had felt some confusion about whether he was organising a trip along a catwalk, or a Broadway musical.

'We'd better kick off rehearsals early, darling,' he had announced, after some breathy deliberation. 'Models are dreadfully dense. I just know I'll need to start them from basics.'

Katrin had not been sure what 'basics' comprised, but the intricate footwork he had sketched had warned that the rehearsals could be lengthy, and traumatic. If she survived the rehearsals! she would be then compéring the evening show.

She was headed for the shower when the doorbell rang. Katrin pulled a silk négligé over her nightgown and sighed. A couple of Indian traders hung around the apartments, forever hopeful that some tenant, sometime, might purchase one of their Oriental rugs and carpets. They worked to an unfathomable timetable. Devotees of the 'hard sell', the Indians were just as likely to ask you to 'feel the quality' at eight a.m. on a Saturday morning, as at some more reasonable hour. But she had no time to waste on a discussion of the merits of Kashkay carpets over those from Qum.

'Not today, thank you,' she announced crisply, allowing the door to open just a crack to prevent the insertion of an Indian toe.

There was a chuckle of amusement, and a low Australian voice asked, 'Remember me, your erstwhile husband?'

Katrin's skin itched all of a sudden. 'What are you doing here?' she asked warily.

'I want to be with you.'

'At eight o'clock in the morning?'

'Why not?'

She tried to find a reason, but failed. 'Where have you come from?' she asked, and opened the door. 'You've never travelled over from Telok Cinta this morning?'

'No, of course not.' Ruark followed her along the hall and into the living room. 'I arrived back in Singapore late yesterday and spent the night at the Regent. My bags are lodged there now.'

'But when are you expected at Barnaby's?'

'Nine o'clock this evening.' Katrin had plopped herself down on the sofa, but he just stood there as if he didn't know what to do next. 'To be honest, I didn't intend to get in touch until after the operation, but——' His shrug indicated he hadn't yet got around to working out why he had. He pushed his hands into his trouser pockets and subjected his feet to an intense scrutiny. 'I didn't get much sleep last night.' He stopped, as if his throat had become constricted. After a long still moment he managed to raise his head and offer a weak smile.

When Ruark's eyes met hers, Katrin recognised a primal need in their blue depths.

'And what?' she coaxed gently.

'I'm scared.' His tongue wetted the edge of his mouth. 'And somehow just being here, with you, comforts me.' At this confession Katrin impulsively rose and wrapped her arms around his neck, but he held himself aloof. 'I—I haven't changed my mind about ... anything,' he said awkwardly. 'Don't interpret this the wrong way.'

'I won't,' she assured him, and rubbed her cheek against his. 'You need comfort, I'll comfort you.'

'Just like that? No strings attached?' he asked, with an air of disbelief.

'Not one.'

'Oh, Kat,' he gulped and drew her close, burying his face in her hair. As he held her, she felt him shudder, and then his tension began to slowly ease. 'Oh, Kat,' he said again, and suddenly they were kissing, hot urgent kisses which gradually propelled them into the bedroom and on to the bed. 'Dear God, you're so beautiful,' Ruark murmured, his hands moving over her as if by compulsion.

'And, purely by chance, I happen to have done as you commanded,' she teased, snuggling closer. 'I've dispensed with underwear.'

She felt the amusement ripple through him. 'So you have.' He gave her a long, easy grin. 'Perhaps I'd better follow suit and dispense with mine. And now,' he murmured, when he returned to lie beside her, 'I intend to take the greatest of pleasure in dispensing with these troublesome layers of silk which lie between me and your silky skin.'

Delicious, blood-tingling minutes were devoted to inching aside her négligé and planting kisses— warm, eager kisses which had her melting into him—on every inch which was revealed. By the time the ribbon straps of her nightgown were slid over her shoulders and the rustling material pulled from her body in tantalising stages, Katrin was dizzy. Her nakedness revealed, she quivered as he pressed his mouth against her skin.

'Now, it's my turn,' she whispered, and raised her lips to the scar on his brow.

Next she kissed his shoulder, rubbing her half-open mouth across the firm muscles, and then bent low to embrace the silver line at his thigh. Ruark groaned. Long tanned fingers were plunged into the dark tumble of her hair, meshing first tightly now slack, again and again until he gave a tortured cry and drew her up beside him. Fiercely he began to kiss her all over again. First her mouth, her throat, her shoulders, and then her breasts, her stomach and along the inner curve of her thigh. Katrin whimpered. Her hips met his and suddenly she was clawing, gasping, writhing, until there came glorious liquifying fusion, and ecstasy was theirs.

Afterwards they lay drowsily together.

'Let's do that all over again,' Ruark murmured, when Katrin stirred herself sufficiently to begin stroking the blue-black furze on his chest.

'Mmm,' she agreed, stretching as he bent to touch her breast with the tip of his tongue. She felt like purring, and was running her fingers languorously through the thick hair at the back of his head when a sudden shrill disturbed the silence. 'The doorbell,' she complained.

When the noise persisted, Ruark raised his head and added some vigorous complaints of his own. 'Can't you let it ring?' he pleaded, as Katrin climbed out of bed to find her négligé. 'Whoever it is, they're bound to get fed up and go eventually if you don't answer.'

'Eventually is the operative word.' She yanked the sash around her waist. 'And before then everyone else on this floor will have been woken up. Two Indians come round hawking carpets, and I know from painful experience that they'll keep a finger on the bell until they receive a reply.'

'Like me to go and hiss something uncomplimentary through the letter-box?' he offered.

She laughed. 'No thanks. If the mouthful I've just heard is a sample, you'll blister the paint.'

Ruark caught hold of her hand. 'Come back quickly, Kat.' His blue eyes clouded, and he held her fast for a moment before he said, 'I'd like us to . . . talk.'

Her spirits soared. 'I'll send the Indians off with fleas in their ears,' she assured him with a wide smile, and shot off towards the front door.

Talk! She hugged the word to her. Ruark wanted to talk. This morning she had sensed a change in him. For the first time she could remember, he was short on detachment and long on need. He was no longer standing on the outside, looking in. So, did talking mean he was ready to change his mind about the future?

For the second time that morning, Katrin opened the door and peeped through the crack, ready with a firm refusal, and for the second time, she gaped. She opened the door wider.

'Good morning, Katrin,' Oliver said, rubbing his hands together. Suave in pale blue shirt, deeper blue cravat, and cavalry twill trousers, he was breezy. 'Dragged you out of bed, have I? I do apologise, but it is——' he examined his watch, 'well after half-past nine. What a lazybones! You're wasting the best part of the day.'

'I can assure you, she hasn't been wasting it,' a deep voice said behind her, and Ruark sauntered along the hall, tucking his shirt into his trousers. His posture and manner was undoubtedly that of the dominant male.

'What's going on?' demanded Oliver. Hawk-eyed, he looked from Katrin in her négligé, to Ruark dressing himself, and back again. 'Why did you allow him to come here? What are you doing?'

Ruark answered before she could speak. 'Use your imagination, sport,' he chuckled. 'What do you think she's doing? Or was doing until you rang that damn bell.'

Oliver raised his horrified gaze to his antagonist. 'But the two of you are divorced!'

'Do you tell him, Katrin, or shall I?' Ruark asked, lounging a broad shoulder against the wall. The question was purely rhetorical, Katrin realised when he allowed her no chance to speak. Instead he gave a wicked grin, and said, 'Sorry if this irritates your ulcer, Ollie, but we're not.'

'Not divorced? You must be!'

'Nope.' Ruark was enjoying himself. 'Seems your pal Beng was a crook. Our divorce never went through.'

Her stepbrother grew rather hot under the collar. 'Rubbish,' he protested. 'I paid the bill.'

'And he took the money and ran. Vanished into the mysterious jungles of Borneo.'

Oliver frowned. 'But Katrin has the decrees.'

'Wrong again. You thought she had them, she thought you had them,' he recited glibly. 'Both living in a fool's paradise. But the bottom line, my dear Ollie, is that no decrees mean no divorce.'

'Do you think I might manage a word in edgeways?' Katrin enquired, looking from one man to the other. They were so involved in their private vendetta that she seemed to have been forgotten.

'But I remember the decrees being itemised on Beng's account,' Oliver continued, deaf to her plea.

'Complete fabrication.' Ruark chopped through the protest like chopping through salami.

'May I speak, please?' Katrin asked, her eyes beginning to spark.

'But Benny Beng's a member of my Rotary Club!' her stepbrother objected.

'Even altar boys have been known to filch the collection,' Ruark smiled.

'But why have you turned up again?' The older man did not say 'like a bad penny'. He had no need to.

Ruark was nonchalant to the extreme. 'Holiday? Trip down memory lane? You choose.'

'*Eeow!*' Katrin yelled, and both of them gazed at her in astonishment. 'Thank you,' she snapped. 'And now that I've managed to attract your attention, I wish to say that I do not like having my private affairs discussed on the doorstep. 'You——' She jabbed Ruark so hard in the ribs that he winced. '——can stop grinning like a Cheshire cat, and you——' Her eyes scorched over Oliver. '——can stop bleating on about paying Beng's bill.' She jerked a thumb which propelled her stepbrother into the hall, then she closed the door and marched off into the living room. 'I reimbursed you for the cost of the divorce ages ago,' she reminded Oliver, as he and Ruark joined her. 'So it's me who's out of pocket, thanks to you recommending a bent solicitor.' She swung to Ruark. 'You can pay the bill next time around. I'm damned if I'm paying twice.'

'Wait a minute.' Oliver was round-eyed. 'Do I understand that you still intend to get a divorce?'

'There's a fifty per cent chance,' she said crisply, ignoring the hesitation on Ruark's face. His hesitation could mean anything or nothing, and Katrin was too impatient for subtleties now.

'Even though the pair of you've just been——' Her stepbrother stuttered to a halt.

She flicked her hair off her shoulders. 'Been in bed together? Yes.'

'You bloody bastard!' Oliver cried, glaring at Ruark, who glared back. 'How dare you fly over here and . . . ingratiate yourself.'

'He hasn't,' Katrin insisted, but she was back to being ignored.

Face beetroot-red, her stepbrother began to twitch nervously, like a prizefighter anxious for the gong to sound at the start of round one. 'I'm going to knock you flat on your back, Lencioni,' he snarled.

'For heaven's sake, Oliver,' she protested. 'You really are overreacting. There's no need for——'

'Let me handle this,' he ordered sharply, and raised two clenched fists.

'Out of the way, Katrin.' Ruark put his hand on her waist to propel her aside. 'I can deal with a wimp like Ollie.'

'Not as effectively as I can deal with you,' his opponent threatened.

Terrified that if a punch landed Ruark's eyes might get hurt, Katrin launched herself forward, arms flailing, and simultaneously hit each man in the stomach as hard as she could. Her blows were unexpected, and thus effective.

'My God!' gasped Oliver, doubling over.

'What the hell was that for?' asked Ruark, wincing.

Katrin disregarded the tingle of her knuckles, and took a deep breath. 'Because I'd like the pair of you to stop this nonsense and listen to what *I* have to say for a change.' She pointed to the sofa. 'Sit,' she ordered, and, like trained dogs, they both sat. Katrin paced the carpet as they recovered. 'I'm fed up to the back teeth with everyone else imagining they can run my life better than me.' She pointed a finger at Oliver, as though picking out the culprit at an identity parade. 'I can manage without your interference for a start. If I choose to welcome Ruark back into my bed, that's entirely my own concern.'

'As your stepbrother——' he began righteously, but received short shrift.

'And in addition to keeping your nose well clear of my private life, in future you don't visit Pivotelle unless it's with my express permission.'

For a moment he seemed bereft of speech, but he quickly recovered. 'Now, Katrin——'

'I don't need to be patronised, or have my authority undermined, and that's what you do. Also I don't need anyone taking sneaky glances at my correspondence, or becoming involved in matters which don't concern them. I'm perfectly capable of running the agency alone.' She paused. 'However, I do appreciate your help with the original financing.'

At last Oliver managed to break in. 'Finance is the reason for my visit this morning,' he announced, speaking at a rush in case she grabbed centre stage again. 'On my return from Antwerp yesterday I telephoned my bank manager, as is my custom, in order to check on several of my investments.'

'Reach the point, Ollie,' Ruark suggested, and stretched into an ostentatious yawn.

'The bank manager told me how Katrin had paid a sizeable cheque into my account,' he completed, shooting a look laced with cyanide.

'That's right,' she confirmed. 'I've cleared your loan.'

'But prematurely,' Oliver admonished, and his

urbane self returned. 'What I want you to do is
take back the money and use it to rent larger
premises. Pivotelle will be able to expand, and
we'll mop up the major part of the Singapore
model market. Can't be bad.'

As he was speaking, Ruark had turned to
monitor Katrin's reaction and when he saw how
her lips jammed together, he chuckled.

'You're way off course, Ollie.'

Katrin swung to him. 'And so are you,' she
snapped, making his brows rise in surprise. 'This
is my territory, keep out.'

He spread his hands, backing off good-
naturedly. 'Yes, ma'am.'

She dealt with her stepbrother. 'I think you've
forgotten that the only reason Pivotelle ever came
into being was because the idea appealed to you
and Daddy. I was undecided.' She gave a
scouring laugh. 'Well, not so much undecided, as
not consulted. But my father couldn't bear the
prospect of me being footloose and fancy free,
because that meant there was always a danger I
might want to up sticks and leave Singapore
without him, and you also preferred me at the
end of a short rope. If memory serves me correct,
the two of you went ahead and fixed the deal in
three seconds' flat.' She circled a hand. 'Hey
presto! One cooked goose.'

'You enjoy working at the agency,' Oliver
protested.

'I do, but the fact remains that Pivotelle
originated oblivious of my wishes. Expansion,
therefore, does not appeal. I'm seriously considering putting the business up for sale.'

'Out of the question,' her stepbrother shot
back.

'Why?' Katrin was ice cool. 'I've settled your loan, for which many thanks, so from now on I'm in total control. The decisions are my responsibility, *mine*.' She inspected her watch. 'And now, would you mind if I asked you to leave? Rehearsals for the hair show are programmed at noon, and before then I must shower, dress and eat breakfast.'

A subdued and thoughtful Oliver rose to his feet. 'I hope the show's a success,' he offered cautiously, as if one false word might find him shot down in flames.

Katrin grinned. 'Thanks. I hope so, too. The only problem is the choreographer, he has delusions of grandeur. I have a nasty suspicion that from noon onwards there's going to be enough hysteria generated to electrify New York.'

Her suspicion was correct. Errol began the session placidly enough, but within half an hour it was clear gentle persuasion was not his forte. His temper began to dicker, his commands grew almost comically shrill.

'Watch me, darlings, watch me!' he pleaded, a gyrating skinny-thin figure in black vest, tights and chunky pink leg-warmers.

The models did watch, often trying not to snigger behind their hands, but watching and doing proved to be two entirely separate propositions. His raw material were not embryo ballet dancers, rather a collection of girls with two left feet. Sweaty-browed, the choreographer persisted, each exhortation a little squeakier than the last, but the hoppity-skips and hip sways he required remained frustratingly elusive. Temperament soaring to prima donna level, he pouted and flounced until the atmosphere threatened to degenerate into a madhouse. Katrin called a halt.

'Errol has an unhappy knack of inspiring giggles,' she commented, giggling herself as she and Ruark found a table in the hotel coffee shop. It was five-thirty, and despite the choreographer's protests, she had sent her girls off. Each had headed for a salon, where stylists were waiting to create miracles. 'When he did that bad imitation of a dying swan and assured us the show would be abysmal, I almost laughed in his face.'

'Abysmal *darlings*,' Ruark corrected, and they exchanged a grin. 'I'm not too happy about the way that guy looks at me,' he confided.

Katrin giggled again. 'Seems like he's taken a shine to you, you'd better keep your back against the wall.' She sobered. 'I can't tell you how much I appreciate your support. If you'd not been there Errol would have boiled over entirely. Most of the girls weren't too bothered by his hysterics, thank goodness, but he is a rather unstable character. It could have been difficult if he'd really let rip.' She frowned. 'It's unfortunate that Lisu didn't find him amusing. She appeared to be on the brink of crumbling several times. If you hadn't intervened at the appropriate time during her tuition and told Errol to cool it, I'm sure she'd have burst into tears.'

'Glad to be of assistance.'

She smiled at him. 'I'm only sorry you've wasted your day. Watching Errol in full flight can hardly be termed inspiring.'

Ruark reached forward to run a finger across

the back of her hand. 'I haven't wasted my time,' he murmured. 'I've been with you.'

Katrin was sensitive to a thrum of emotion in his voice, and wondered if now was the right time to 'talk'. She was deciding she would raise the subject of the future when a waitress appeared. The opportunity was lost.

'I'm keeping my fingers crossed that Lisu doesn't decide to abscond,' she said, when their orders had been taken. 'Suppose she takes a fit of the vapours and doesn't return for the show?'

'She'll return. She has a strong sense of loyalty towards you and Pivotelle. Lisu and I had a little chat, while you were otherwise engaged,' Ruark explained. 'Timid she might be, but she's determined not to let anyone down.'

Katrin suddenly remembered the DeSouza competition. She was in the middle of explaining Lisu's entry and the ramifications, when their order of Chicken Kiev arrived. 'So what do I do if Lisu happens to win? There's bound to be charges of double-dealing, with me at Pivotelle and you working for the advertising company.'

'Shrieks of collusion,' he agreed. 'And I do rather more than work there, I'm a partner now.' He grinned at her surprise. 'Which makes for an even stickier situation. Why did you enter her in the first place? It was stupid. Even if we'd been divorced——'

'I didn't,' she said hastily. 'Oliver did. Behind my back.'

Ruark gave a grunt of exasperation. 'Lisu's a good-looking girl. Great skin, good bones, she must be in with a chance. Does she photograph well?'

'Like a dream.' Katrin was gloomy. 'You

couldn't intervene, could you? Make a phone call and have her portfolio whisked away?'

'Doubtful. Being on holiday, I'm out of touch, but I'd say it's almost certain the cream of the crop have already been passed on to DeSouza for their consideration.'

'But if Lisu's chosen and is promptly disqualified, Mrs Ho will have my guts for garters.' She shuddered at the prospect.

'Let's not cross bridges,' he soothed. 'Photogenic or not, Lisu would still have to attend a personal interview if she was on the short-list. And if her nerves showed through, that would count against her.'

'But her looks are so damn perfect,' Katrin complained, and she did not feel any better when Ruark agreed.

A darting figure in black rushed into vision as they were drinking coffee.

'Katrin, darling,' Errol pleaded, taking time off to preen for a moment when he noticed curious glances from other diners. 'Could you come and have a word with the management? They've brought in huge pots of oleander for the stage, but they're red, *red*! Pink I could have accepted, white would have been perfect, but red!'

Ruark tried not to smile. 'Come along, pussycat,' he said, pushing back his chair. 'Looks like you're back in action.'

She diverted the crisis by swapping the oleander for pink and white calliandra. Happy once more, Errol made a great performance of instructing the porters on precisely where the pots must be positioned. But minutes later a problem erupted over the sound system, and then the choreographer became uptight about the placing of the publicity material. By the time Katrin went to change, she felt the sooner the entire evening was over, the better. All her persuasive powers had been needed to keep Errol from exploding, and if Ruark, with his humourous asides, hadn't been close at hand she felt sure Errol's hysteria would have proved infectious and she would have succumbed to a spot of ranting and raving herself.

In the quiet of the changing room, she had a chance to rally. Her models were wearing identical Grecian gowns in white silk, but her outfit was a white silk tunic over tight trousers. The narrow belt around her waist was gold, and so were her high-heeled sandals. She had brought a golden head-band from home, and once her face had been made-up and her hair brushed into shiny waves, she tied the band in place across her brow.

In due course the models started to arrive back. Competition to be noticed was hot among the salons, and each girl's hairstyle, often decorated with gems and feathers, was more flamboyant than the last. In time the stylists drifted in, clutching curling tong and combs, ready for last-minute touches once their particular girl had dressed. The area adjacent to the changing rooms had been equipped with chairs and mirrors, and the whole place began to hum.

By the time Katrin joined Ruark beside the door on to the ballroom, the guests were sat at the tables chatting and quaffing first drinks.

'Lisu hasn't shown up yet,' she fretted. 'And there's no sign of Jerry, her hairdresser, either.'

He checked his watch. 'Don't panic, pussycat. There's still plenty of time.'

But an hour later, when the guests had eaten their hors-d'oeuvres and were halfway through the *Faisan à la Crème*, Lisu had still not returned. Despite Ruark's efforts to calm her, Katrin's alarm grew. She interrupted Errol's skittish conversation with one of the hair stylists and took him to one side.

'Suppose we needed to cut out a segment?' she asked, attempting to feed him the idea as though it was blancmange and not dynamite. 'Would one part of the show be easily eliminated?'

The choreographer looked horrified. 'Impossible! The music is cued. Alter anything and you'll ruin the entire performance.'

'Then I'm afraid there's a chance it might have to be ruined,' Ruark said firmly, coming to stand at Katrin's shoulder. 'Don't bust a gut, but there's a possibility Lisu has opted out.'

'The silly bitch!' Errol squawked. 'Doesn't she realise this evening is a showcase for my talents? She's going to destroy me, destroy me.'

'Your hypercriticism this afternoon wouldn't have helped her state of mind,' Ruark pointed out.

Errol was bristling at this blunt honesty, when he suddenly looked behind him. His face lit up into a smile. 'Saved in the nick of time!'

Katrin swivelled. A girl with a kinked-wire tangle of platinum-blonde hair was approaching.

'What do you think, Mrs Lencioni?' the girl beneath the hair asked. 'Hasn't Jerry done a marvellous job?'

Her gesture drew attention to a slender Chinese youth, armed with hair-dryer and collection of brushes.

'Lisu?' Katrin cleared her throat and started

again, one note lower. 'Lisu, what have you done? Your mother'll go mad.'

The girl's face fell, but only for an instant. 'Mother's always telling me I must be positive, and I have been.' She twirled around, displaying the bird's nest from all angles. 'I'm the new Lisu Ho,' she exclaimed, and tripped off to change.

'Dear God!' Ruark breathed, as she disappeared. 'One thing's for certain. You need have no worries now about her winning the DeSouza competition. A shock-haired blonde doesn't stand a chance. If the judges do call her for interview after studying her portfolio, they're going to get a big surprise.'

Katrin tried to come to terms with what she had just seen.

'Even though she's gorgeous, she looks distinctly oddball. That mix of Asian features and platinum hair is ... different.' She shrugged. 'Still, if her new look gives her confidence, maybe it's worthwhile.'

He shook his head. 'I'd be amazed if true confidence can be acquired merely by bleaching your hair.'

Unfortunately Ruark was proved correct. By the time Lisu had donned her Grecian gown, her exuberance had fallen a notch. And despite Jerry's delighted chatter as he stuck sequins and ornaments into the platinum puffball, she began to suffer withdrawal symptoms. She ceased to talk. Her face paled. The fingers started their twisting.

'Stagefright, I'm afraid,' Ruark whispered, as he and Katrin listened to the opening address. A director had flown over from Germany especially for the evening's events, and was now plugging his company's products as hard as he could.

'What if she backs out at the crucial moment?' Katrin whispered back.

She could well imagine the running duel which was taking place in Lisu's head. She would be desperate to do her best, had a horror of spoiling the show, but—— Blonde and kinked though she was, nothing had changed internally. She was still shy, still timid, still insecure.

'Lisu will be on stage,' Ruark said reassuringly, as the director came to the end of his speech. 'She won't let you down.'

Katrin wished she had his faith, but she had no more time in which to fret for the director had begun to introduce her as the compère. She braced herself to take over the microphone.

The director swung an arm. 'And now, may I hand you over to our lady from Pivotelle, Mrs Katrin Lencioni.'

She stepped forward into a round of applause. After briefly welcoming the guests, she paused. By arrangement, the ballroom lights were dimmed, and a murmur of delighted approval came as flashes of electric pink, white and violet lit up the room. A pinprick of bright light swung to the start of the catwalk and slowly expanded. There was Roselind, her head crested by a gleaming wave of bird-black hair studded with diamante. A twang of electronic beat came from the sound system. The show was on.

Everything started amazingly well. The models who had clumped and stumbled that afternoon now transformed themselves into chorus girls. They stepped to the music, swayed when they should, and as each one paraded there was a

prolonged round of applause. From the corner of
her eye, Katrin saw Errol start to snap his fingers
and smile.

Three-quarters of the way through, and all was
glossy success. The audience was riveted, the
models continued to excel, and the German
director had given her a joyous 'thumbs up' sign.
But the final girl to appear was Lisu! Katrin's
fingers tightened around the microphone. When
Errol had declared the show would be ruined if
anything was altered, he had been speaking the
truth. She knew the music was so tightly
synchronised that any gap—let alone three
minutes when the catwalk remained unoccupied—
would be recognised in a trice. How could she fill
the gap if Lisu failed to appear?

The ninth girl, hair cleverly tinted with streaks
of blue and green, pranced into the spotlight, and
exited three minutes later to whistles and cheers.
Katrin darted a worried glance sideways. By
rights Lisu should be stationed there in the
gloom, ready to take her place. The doorway was
deserted! Had she bolted from the hotel in terror?
Locked herself in the loo, and was refusing to
come out? Katrin's gaze skittered wildly around,
searching for Ruark. But he couldn't help her, no
matter how much he sympathised. She was the
stooge coupled to the microphone, stood alone
before an audience of hundreds. She was the one
who must paper over that three-minute gap.
Katrin gulped. What did she say when the
pinpoint of light, now travelling into position,
widened to reveal sweet nothing? Hectic thought
was undertaken. Switching immediately to the
finale was out, because the music would be wrong
and the other models would be taken unawares.

No, she must keep her head and offer some
general commentary. What commentary? Already
she had spoken in glowing and detailed terms
about the hair products and the hair stylists, so
what else could she say? Three minutes became
three years.

The music leapt into a fresh rhythm. The
pinpoint of light stopped and began to slowly
swell. It grew and grew. Grew on an empty
space. Katrin could feel the surprise in the
ballroom, feel the hairs stand up on the back of
her neck. She set her shoulders and, as her pulses
moved into top gear, she opened her mouth to
speak.

Two people landed in the spotlight, a giggling
blonde and a tall young man with blue-black hair.
Wide-eyed, Katrin watched as Ruark calmly
tucked Lisu's arm under his and waltzed her with
him along the catwalk. The audience, presuming
this change of format to be planned, burst into
applause. Ruark grinned down at his partner, and
she, taking strength from his smile, grinned back.
Panic over. Holding Lisu by the hand, Ruark
treated her to a short snatch of disco-dancing
before the three-minute span ended and they
disappeared into darkness.

The moment the finale ended, Katrin fell into
his arms.

'Thank you, thank you,' she babbled with
relief. 'I was so flabbergasted when you and
Lisu appeared, I almost forgot to read my
notes. Though I don't think anyone would have
noticed if I hadn't said a word. They were all
too busy watching you do your John Travolta
bit.'

Ruark pulled a face. 'I can assure you, only

sheer necessity prompted me to make a stage début.'

'What happened?'

'I'd decided it would be prudent to keep an eye on Lisu,' he explained. 'And I saw that as each model took their turn, she was degenerating into a nervous wreck. By the time her entrance was imminent, she was virtually rooted to the spot. There was no time for comforting encouragement, so I just grabbed and bundled her into the ballroom. I had no intention of accompanying her into the limelight, but she clung on to me so damned tight that there was no alternative.'

'You helped me out of a very tight spot,' Katrin smiled, and reached up to dab a kiss on the end of his nose. 'For which I'm truly grateful.'

'I'm only returning the favour, pussycat.'

She gave a puzzled frown. 'How?'

'Ever since eight o'clock this morning, you've been helping me out of a tight spot.'

'But for the most part you've only been hanging around the rehearsals,' she protested.

'I've been with you.' His grin was lopsided. 'Sorry to be repetitious, but that's all that matters right now. Dear God!' he suddenly exclaimed. 'I was due at Barnaby's over half an hour ago.'

'I'll run you round in the car.'

He shook his head. 'You're too involved here. You must stay. That German director is itching to buy you a congratulatory drink. Don't bother about me. All I need to do is collect my suitcase from the Bell Captain and ask him to call me a taxi.'

Katrin felt confused and aimless. There had been no opportunity to talk, no opportunity for

Ruark to explain how he had had a change of mind. But if he had changed his mind, if he had wanted her to remain his wife come what may, surely he would have *made* an opportunity?

'I'll visit you tomorrow, after the operation,' she said, looking anywhere but at him. 'When is it scheduled?'

'Early afternoon.' Ruark looked thoughtful. 'But could you come round to Barnaby's tomorrow morning? We really must talk.'

Straight from her misery, she was pinnacle high. 'Talk?' She acted casual, afraid to reveal the excitement which was chasing through her veins.

He nodded. 'About the past.'

'The past?'

Katrin hit an all-time low. To hell with the past! The past didn't matter any more. She wanted to talk about the future, a *shared* future.

CHAPTER NINE

KATRIN drove so slowly that more than once she incurred the noisy frustration of other road-users, but she still arrived at Barnaby's well before visiting was allowed. She was forced to spend an edgy thirty minutes leafing through out-of-date magazines in the waiting room, while her eye constantly checked the sluggardly progress of the clock. When a nurse appeared to give her the go-ahead, she leapt into action like a startled gazelle.

Ruark had a room on the third floor, and when she reached his door, she hesitated. All the strength had drained from her. Katrin took a deep breath, knocked and stepped inside. The smile she had pasted on, came unstuck. What she had expected, she did not know, but to discover Ruark in bed with a thick white bandage wrapped around his eyes made tears well uncontrollably.

'It's me,' she gulped.

His talk of eye problems had had a curiously theoretical and distant quality, she realised, but now her reaction was acute. The impact of what was involved hit her. Fear was paramount. Fear of Ruark being in pain. Fear of him—such a fine man—spending the remainder of his life wandering through a dimly lit landscape. To see him bound up like a wounded soldier made her want to weep and rail at life for being unjust. But if she started to weep, would she ever stop?

He grinned as she neared the bed. 'I know it's you, I can smell you.'

She followed his lead, there was no alternative. 'That's nice!' she protested chirpily.

'You're wearing that *Le Must de* something or other Ollie buys each Christmas.'

'Now that's perception for you!' She resolved to hide her distress. 'Are you okay?'

'I'm fine. Forgive the blindfold, but I've been given some special drops and now my eyes must be kept covered until the magnetism takes place.' He held out his hand and groped to find hers. When their fingers interlaced, he tugged her closer. 'What about a good morning kiss, pussycat?'

Katrin managed a quick lurch at his mouth. If Ruark held her too close, or too long, she would burst into tears.

'Being Sunday morning the shops are closed, so I'm afraid I could find neither grapes nor the latest *Playboy*,' she quipped.

'Curses.' His amusement was brief, for his jaw took on a determined slant. 'We must talk about the past, about what went wrong.'

'Why?' She brought a chair up to the bedside and sat down, fidgeting with the buttons of her khaki cotton jacket. 'At the end of a talk nothing will have changed, so what's the point?'

'Call it therapy. Call it self-help. I need to bring our marriage out into the open. We've never discussed basics, not really, and I'd like everything cut and dried in my mind.'

The old detached Ruark had returned! But Katrin could not be so detached. She was too emotionally wound up in the present to welcome a dispassionate look at days gone by.

'Well, I wouldn't.' She thrust her jacket over the back of the chair. Now she was a summer-girl, in sleeveless shirt of white and scarabee stripes, and short khaki skirt. 'I don't believe in taking watches to pieces just to see how they work.' She looked around for a bell. 'Is there any chance of rounding up a cup of coffee?'

'The coffee here is lousy, like an Armenian tram driver's bathwater,' he declared. Blindfolded he might be, but his humour was still bright-eyed.

'Have you ever drunk an Armenian tram driver's bathwater?' Katrin responded.

'Every Shrove Tuesday since I was knee-high, and don't try and sidetrack. I have a pretty shrewd idea why you refused to join me in Hong Kong, but I need an explanation in your own words.'

'What's done is done,' she said testily. 'The past can't be changed.'

'It can be explained,' Ruark insisted. 'Some couples are born to be divorced, others have divorce thrust upon them. My bet is the latter applies to us.'

Katrin folded her arms. 'Are you talking about the past, or the future?' she asked pointedly.

He refused to rise to the bait. 'The past, that's all that interests me right this minute. Look, if you'd rather, I'll go first.' He appeared to have rehearsed all his lines, for when he spoke, he was fluent. 'Fifteen months ago I dished out my ultimatum, breezed off to Hong Kong and fully expected you to join me. When you didn't, I amazed myself by falling to pieces. Up to that point I'd regarded myself as a tough guy, with a skin you could strike matches on.'

'You still are,' she interrupted, and he heard her resentment.

'Okay, I deserve that. The point I'm trying to make is that I never realised how much I needed you until it was too late.' Ruark rubbed roughly at his jaw. 'What you said about me never caring too much, was fair comment. I cared for Dick, and look what happened to him. After he was killed, I think maybe I was too frightened to put my emotions on the line a second time. Maybe I subconsciously believed that if I gave you everything, I'd lose you.'

'You *did* lose me,' she said impatiently.

'Yes.' He gave an odd laugh. 'But by that time any kind of dependence seemed to be a form of weakness.'

Like it or not, Katrin was tempted to become involved.

'If that's what you felt, then I understand why you resented my father's attitude to life so much. He was the other side of the coin.'

'Felix certainly believed in close, close relationships,' Ruark agreed with a wry smile.

'Total dependence,' she said, redefining his comment.

'He did have a need to consult everyone else on all aspects of his life. I used to get so rattled because he never reached an opinion on his own. And the number of times he'd say, 'Oliver, do you mind if——', even if he just wanted a window left open!' Ruark shook his head in bewilderment.

'He set my teeth on edge, too. But Daddy was never happier than when he was playing the self-appointed role of second fiddle.'

'That's not criticism, is it?' he derided. 'What's happened to that mutual admiration society of yours? If I ever dared make a comment about

Felix's shortcomings in the past, you were on me like a ton of bricks.'

'I was being loyal.'

'Painfully so.'

'I admit I did leap on to the defensive rather too rapidly, but you were so damned capable and he was so ... incapable. I needed to protect him.'

Ruark's brow creased. 'Did you?'

'Yes. You've always misinterpreted our relationship. You saw the parent and the child, and imagined our roles were the usual ones.'

'But they weren't?'

Katrin sat up a little straighter. 'No. Daddy hugged me close, I grant you that, but not to save me from the world, to save himself. I've often wondered if, when my mother died, some vital spark went out of him. But maybe Daddy never did possess any grit, maybe he was always just clay.' She gave a self-despising laugh. 'I was so grateful when Muriel swooped on him. Selfishly, I hoped he'd transfer the weight of his affections to her.'

'And did he?' Ruark asked, fascinated, it seemed, by what she was telling him.

'In part, but after Muriel died he switched back to me, plus some. He damn near smothered me.'

He scratched his nose. 'I never knew you felt like this about Felix.'

'I hardly knew myself until after he died. I realise how cruel this sounds, but once he'd gone it was as if a great weight had been lifted off my shoulders. Don't get me wrong,' she said hastily, 'I loved my father and I certainly didn't want him to die, but——' She broke off in confusion.

'God! I'm heartless. There was poor Daddy doting on me, and I found it claustrophobic.'

'I understand what you mean,' Ruark said slowly. 'Now that you've said all this I can see that, to a large extent, Felix lived his life through you. You coloured his world. If you were happy, he was happy.'

'And vice versa.'

'How did Felix react when I went off to Hong Kong?' he asked, full of curiosity.

Katrin glanced at him, only to think how odd it was not to be able to see his eyes.

'Like you say, Daddy took his cue from me. I knew if he guessed how broken up I was, he'd take my troubles upon himself and pull us both down into a sea of despondency, so——' She shrugged. 'I acted the merry optimist. I pretended to take our separation in my stride.'

Ruark's finger traced an aimless pattern on the sheet.

'You do know I wrote to Felix?'

'Yes.'

'I pinned so many hopes on that letter.' His laugh was supposed to be airy, but belly-flopped. 'Didn't you consider I beckoned seductively enough?'

'I only came across the letter last week,' she explained. 'The envelope was tucked into the lining of that old leather writing case. I found it by accident.'

'You only read it last week? Felix never told you I'd written?' He changed his question into a statement and pounded a fist on the bed. 'Felix never told you I'd written, dammit. Dear God! I've been so stupid. I'd presumed he'd shown you the letter, but now I see that wouldn't have been his way at all. Your father would have been bound to consult Ollie first. Doubtless your darling stepbrother convinced him how you should be spared the misfortune of linking up again with a penny-poor sailor, at all costs.'

Katrin considered the matter. 'I don't think so. I can be a plausible actress when I try, and I tried! It's more likely my father believed I was happy without you and settled for the status quo.'

'Which tied in with his subconscious belief that his need of you superseded my need of you?'

'He might not have admitted that to himself, but it could have been true,' she agreed.

Ruark gave a dry laugh. 'Then Felix should have witnessed the hell I went through. He'd have soon realised I was just as dependent on your love as he was.'

'But why didn't you come back much earlier, if you felt so rotten about our break-up?'

'For a variety of reasons.' He gave a long drawn-out sigh. 'All of which sound impossibly frail now, but which made vast common sense at the time. To start with, I was determined I wouldn't return until I had money in the bank. Pride meant I needed to be able to offer you a decent standard of living. A second reason was that I was forever hopeful of the company moving me to a settled base. I thought if I stopped flitting around like a blue-backed fly, we'd stand a far better chance. It was important that we started off again with everything exactly right.'

'You were still the idealist who insisted on a virgin on his wedding night?'

Ruark laughed. 'I guess so. And then there were the not so noble reasons, like I was scared to death that even when I'd assembled the money and the home-based package, you might not want to resume our married life.' He tugged at the eye bandage. 'Also I wanted to punish you for not joining me, especially after I'd sent you that damned letter! But my feelings bewildered me. At one and the same time I wanted to rush back and blubber an apology, but I needed to wait until all the signs were propitious, propitious from my point of view.'

'But what kind of an existence did you have during the months in Hong Kong and the States and Australia, while you were waiting for the signs?'

He gave a grin of cheeky self-contempt. 'I channelled all my energies, sexual and otherwise, into my career. As you know, I'm a partner now, so it paid off. But unfortunately even such lofty people as partners in international advertising agencies feel guilty and ashamed and rebellious, and God knows what else.'

'That sounds familiar.'

'It does?'

Katrin nodded. 'I've worked my way through a ragbag of emotions, too.' She had not intended to contribute to this inspection of the past, but suddenly there was the conviction that if she explained how she had felt, she would be cleansed. 'For various reasons, I was reluctant to buy an air ticket and shoot off after you into the unknown. Firstly, I was uneasy about leaving my father, it smacked of desertion. And moving to live in a strange country is a major decision for anyone! I found it all too much to absorb on the spur of the moment.' Her chin lifted. 'Added to which you hadn't exactly described our new life in Hong Kong as being one which would flow with milk and honey. You painted a very grim picture.'

'Okay.'

She frowned. 'Okay what?'

'Okay, I concede your point, but the reason I emphasised the drawbacks was because I refused to offer you a rose garden when one didn't exist.'

'But you didn't just emphasise the drawbacks, you spelled them out in scarlet letters six foot high, and you underlined them!'

'I wanted to be honest,' he protested. 'I don't believe in glossing over problems. I was desperate to save you from any disappointment.'

'But it was overkill,' Katrin insisted. 'You frightened me half to death, you frightened Daddy half to death, and you provided Oliver with a wealth of ammunition. He quoted back your words a thousand times. How I wouldn't know a single soul. How we'd be living in downmarket conditions. How you'd travel constantly and I'd be a grass widow.'

'Yet you didn't refuse to join me just because you were frightened?' he asked thoughtfully. 'That doesn't sound like you.'

'No,' she admitted. 'Fear of the unknown was something I could tackle, but I needed time to sort out my priorities. I accepted my allegiance was to you, but I wanted to ease myself out of my father's life, not rip away.' Katrin bit into her lip. 'However, you demanded an instant decision and—I know I was being childish—but at first I decided I could be as stubborn as you. When you left, I was convinced you were bluffing and that you'd soon be back. I was sure you'd feel we had enough going for us to warrant a second chance.'

'And what fool idea made you inaugurate a divorce?' he asked, and his voice was harsh.

'You never telephoned. As far as I was aware, you never wrote,' she retaliated. 'And I was too used to having my own way, I suppose. I decided I'd shock you into returning. I imagined that the day the divorce papers were delivered, was the day you'd get the first flight back.' Katrin gave a little grunt. 'But Benny Beng outwitted me. No papers, no husband.'

'Yet you allowed the divorce to run full course,' he reminded her coldly. 'As you thought.'

'That was a mistake.' Her sigh sounded very much like a sob. 'I presumed there'd be plenty of time in which to call a halt. The reason I left the divorce proceedings to take care of themselves was because I didn't want to do anything to hurry them along. If they took a year, fine! I never intended to go as far as a legal separation. But Daddy had his stroke and when I surfaced from that, everything was over. I realise now that Oliver had been pushing like mad behind the scenes.' Katrin gave another sob-sigh. 'And Ruark, there's something else I don't intend to do. After your operation——'

'Wait.' His tongue flicked the corner of his mouth. 'You remember at Telok Cinta how I was being very macho and protective?'

'And demeaning,' Katrin added, her voice cracking.

'Um, well.' Ruark rubbed his jaw, fussed with his bandage, rubbed his jaw again. 'It appears I'm not quite the macho man I thought I was. I don't know which animal instinct landed me on your doorstep yesterday morning,

but once I was with you it sure as hell felt
good.' He stretched out his hand, wanting to
touch her. 'I don't think I could have survived
yesterday without you, Kat,' he said huskily, as
her fingers slid between his. He tightened his
grip. 'And I don't think I can manage to get
through the rest of my life without you. What's
more, I can't seem to drum up the slightest
inclination to try.' He attempted a laugh. 'We
both know I'm a stubborn cuss who hates to
change his mind, and we both know that by the
end of today I may not have too much left by
way of potential, but even so——'

Katrin leant forward to stop his words with a
kiss. 'But even so, I'm sticking to my husband
and you're sticking to your wife.' She kissed him
again. 'And that's final.'

'Yes, Mrs Lencioni, ma'am,' Ruark agreed.
There was an accompanying naval salute, but all
hopes of nautical toughness were defeated when a
tear appeared from beneath his bandage and
trickled down his chin.

Back home, Katrin threw herself down on the
bed and sobbed non-stop for an hour. Afterwards
she dried her face, took a shower, ate lunch, and
felt much better. Meeting the future together, no
matter how many problems it held, was infinitely
better than meeting it alone.

Because the opthalmologist had suggested she
delay her return until Ruark was well clear of the
operation and any anaesthetic, she forced herself
to remain away from Barnaby's as long as she
possibly could, but by seven o'clock she could
wait no longer. Katrin swung the Ford into a
parking space outside the hospital, grabbed her

bag of grapes—for which she had scoured the city—and sped to the third floor.

She paused outside Ruark's room to give herself a short lecture. She was not to cry and upset him. She must be brave. She must be optimistic—she was good at that. She must keep cool.

Anxious not to wake him if he was asleep, she peeped cautiously round the door. What she saw made her heart sing. Ruark was out of bed, his back to her as he stood by the window. He had taken off his pyjama jacket, and his skin, so deeply tanned, gleamed in the light. He looked so healthy, so virile, and there was no bandage wrapped around his head!

'Hello,' she said.

'Katrin?'

He turned and nervous tension tightened her stomach, dismay weakened her knees. There was no bandage wrapped *around* his head, but pads of white lint were taped across his eyes. A desperate flurry of panic dislodged every single one of her good resolutions. Shedding grapes and handbag somewhere along the way, Katrin flew into his arms, showering him with assurances, telling him she loved him, saying everything would be all right.

Ruark held her close, and kissed her hair.

'But it *is* all right, Kat. The particles have been removed. The magnetism was successful.'

She jerked back, frightened to believe. 'Successful?'

'The reason for the padding is because my eyes are rather sensitive to the light right now. But tomorrow morning they'll be back to normal, and I'll be discharged. And that means

no more Armenian tram driver's bathwater,
thank God!'

If he hadn't been holding her, she would have
fallen down at his feet with relief. The threats
had gone. Wiped out. Vanished.

'Every single particle's been removed?' she
checked, needing the wonderful news to be
repeated.

'Every single one. The opthalmologist said that
because I'm as healthy as a rampant bull——'

Katrin remembered what a prim old maid the
opthalmologist had seemed. 'He said that?' she
asked in surprise.

Ruark grinned. 'Am I so transparent? Okay, he
said I was healthy. I added the bull. And, believe
me, the way I'm feeling right now, it fits. But to
return to my health. He said my general good
health made the particles simpler to remove, firm
eye muscles or something. He also says that
now I should have no problems whatsoever
with my eyesight—at least, not until I'm a
grandfather.'

She placed the tip of her finger on his
cheekbone and traced a line. 'When are you
planning on becoming a grandfather?' she
queried softly.

'After I've become a father.' He waited until
her finger neared the corner of his mouth, then,
by virtue of a quick jerk, managed to grab and
suck at the fingertip.

'But could your wife cope with becoming a
mother?' she asked, straight-faced. 'Surely a hot-
house plant could never manage alone? She'd
require wet nurses and nannies and——'

'I've changed my mind about that, too,' Ruark
mumbled, trying to nibble at another of her

fingers. 'Anyone who hits blokes in the stomach like you did yesterday, has to be able to cope with a baby or two. And their father.'

Katrin took her hand away from his mouth. 'Him I can cope with, standing on my head.'

'How about lying on your back?'

'Ruark,' she said warily, alert to the mischief tugging at the corner of his mouth.

'They say if you're deprived of one of your senses, the others compensate, and it's true. I've never known that perfume of yours smell so delicious, nor your fingers taste so good. And do you think it's because I'm unable to see that I feel so horribly—or is it beautifully—horny?'

'I've no idea.' She caught hold of the hand which had begun to smooth a way along her thigh, and held it firm. 'I think it's time you went back to bed, Mr Lencioni.'

'So do I, but you come, too.'

'I will not!'

'Katrin, my love,' he said persuasively. 'I'm paying through the nose for these facilities.'

She laughed. 'Paying through the nose for Armenian tram driver's bathwater?'

Ruark raised his head and spoke to an invisible observer. 'The girl talks coffee, the girl talks sidetrack. As I said, the cost of this room and bed would make Rockefeller think twice, so I know a very good way to get value for money.'

'I'm sure you do.' Katrin was brimming over with happiness.

'And we have an awful lot of time to catch up on,' he pointed out.

She kissed him. 'We'll make a start tomorrow.'

'Promise?'

She placed her finger on the dragon's head and slowly traced her way down a shoulder muscle, a forearm, a wrist.

'I do,' she said. 'Oh, Ruark. I do, I do, I do.'

ANNE MATHER

Anne Mather, one of Harlequin's leading
romance authors, has published more
than 100 million copies worldwide,
including **Wild Concerto,**
a *New York Times* best-seller.

Catherine Loring was an
innocent in a South
American country beset by
civil war. Doctor Armand
Alvares was arrogant
yet compassionate.
They could not ignore
the flame of love igniting
within them…whatever
the cost.

HIDDEN IN THE FLAME

Harlequin reaches into the hearts and minds of women across America to bring you

Harlequin American Romance™

Enter a uniquely exciting
new world with

Harlequin
American Romance T.M.

Harlequin American Romances are the first romances to explore today's love relationships. These compelling novels reach into the hearts and minds of women across America... probing the most intimate moments of romance, love and desire.

You'll follow romantic heroines and irresistible men as they boldly face confusing choices. Career first, love later? Love without marriage? Long-distance relationships? All the experiences that make love real are captured in the tender, loving pages of **Harlequin American Romances.**

What makes American women so different when it comes to love? Find out with **Harlequin American Romance!**

Send for your introductory FREE book now!

PASSIONATE!
CAPTIVATING!
SOPHISTICATED!

Harlequin Presents...

**The favorite fiction
of women the world over!**

Beautiful contemporary romances that
touch every emotion of a woman's heart—
passion and joy, jealousy and heartache...
but most of all...love.

Fascinating settings in the exotic
reaches of the world—
from the bustle of an international capital
to the paradise of a tropical island.

**All this and much, much more
in the pages of**

Harlequin Presents...

**Wherever paperback books are sold, or through
Harlequin Reader Service**

In the U.S.	In Canada
2504 West Southern Avenue	P.O. Box 2800, Postal Station A
Tempe, AZ 85282	5170 Yonge Street
	Willowdale, Ontario M2N 5T5

**No one touches the heart of a woman
quite like Harlequin!**